She stepped through the door. "I am your employee. I have a contract that affords me rights."

The door almost closed in his face. Almost as put out at her failure to hold it open for him as he was by this bolshy attitude, which, even by Victoria's standards, went beyond minor insubordination, Marcello decided it was time to remind her who the actual boss was and of her obligations to him.

"You cannot say you were not warned of what the job entailed when you agreed to take it," he said when he caught up with her in the living room. She was already at the door that would take her through to the reception room. "It is why you are given such a handsome salary and generous perks."

Instead of going through the door, she came to a stop and turned back around, folding her arms across her breasts. "Quite honestly, Marcello, the way I'm feeling right now, I'd give the whole lot up for one lie-in. One lousy lie-in. That's all I wanted, but you couldn't even afford me that, could you? I tell you what, stuff your *handsome salary and generous perks*—I quit."

Michelle Smart's love affair with books started when she was a baby and would cuddle them in her cot. A voracious reader of all genres, she found her love of romance established when she stumbled across her first Harlequin book at the age of twelve. She's been reading them—and writing them—ever since. Michelle lives in Northamptonshire, England, with her husband and two young smarties.

Books by Michelle Smart

Harlequin Presents

Claiming His Baby at the Altar
Innocent's Wedding Day with the Italian
Christmas Baby with Her Ultra-Rich Boss
Cinderella's One-Night Baby

Scandalous Royal Weddings

Crowning His Kidnapped Princess
Pregnant Innocent Behind the Veil
Rules of Their Royal Wedding Night

A Billion-Dollar Revenge

Bound by the Italian's "I Do"

The Greek Groom Swap

The Forbidden Greek

The Diamond Club

Heir Ultimatum

Visit the Author Profile page at Harlequin.com for more titles.

RESISTING THE BOSSY BILLIONAIRE

MICHELLE SMART

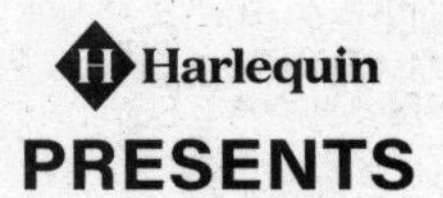

PRESENTS

Recycling programs for this product may not exist in your area.

ISBN-13: 978-1-335-93935-7

Resisting the Bossy Billionaire

Harlequin Enterprises ULC
22 Adelaide St. West, 41st Floor
Toronto, Ontario M5H 4E3, Canada
www.Harlequin.com

Printed in Lithuania

RESISTING THE BOSSY BILLIONAIRE

To my wonderful mum. You're one in a million xxx

CHAPTER ONE

'THE IMPERIAL MARCH' pierced Victoria Cusack's consciousness.

Muttering a curse, she rolled over and flapped her hand on her bedside table, fingers groping for her phone.

Accepting the call, she stuck the phone to her ear and peered through bleary eyes at her bedside alarm clock. It was five a.m.

'What's wrong?' she mumbled as she pulled her lovely warm duvet back up to her chin. It had better be an emergency. Nothing less than broken limbs would count.

'Patrick and Christina are ill.'

She blinked the sleep away. 'What's wrong with them?'

'A virus. They have to isolate and I can't work the coffee machine.'

She groaned. Her boss lived in a loft apartment in one of Manhattan's most exclusive buildings overlooking Central Park. She had no idea why he bothered paying the twenty-four-hour concierge service fees seeing as he never used it. 'I'll get coffee delivered to you.'

'No, I need you to come and make it for me.'

She gritted her teeth tightly before relaxing her mouth into an irritated sigh. 'It's Sunday.'

'You can still take the rest of the day off if you like.'

'How kind.'

Sarcasm was wasted on Marcello Guardiola. 'I'll add a bonus to your salary.'

Victoria didn't want a bonus. She wanted the lie-in she'd been looking forward to.

Friends and family back home in Ireland thought her job was glamorous? Ha!

'I'll throw some clothes on and come over.'

'I've woken you up?'

She rolled her eyes and pulled a face. 'Yes, Marcello, you've woken me up.'

She didn't expect an apology and none was forthcoming. 'More hours of the day to enjoy. See you in ten.'

The line went dead before she could correct him and say she'd be there in twenty minutes, not ten.

Muttering under her breath, she threw her thick duvet off then immediately pulled it back over herself. Good heavens, it was *freezing*.

Only by imagining personally maiming Marcello could she coax her protesting body out of bed and her feet onto the frigid floor. Storm Brigit was due to hit the East Coast that day, and a quick peek out of her curtains proved her suspicions that the expected snow had already started to fall.

A quick brush of her hair, a longer brush of her teeth

and then, shivering, she stripped off her flannelette py-jamas and dressed in thick tights covered by fitted black jeans, thermal socks, and a black vest top that she cov-ered with a grey cashmere jumper. Black snow boots, black woolly hat, thick knitted black scarf and then her padded, faux-fur-lined khaki winter coat and leather gloves all donned, phone shoved in coat pocket, and she was ready to go.

Down three flights of stairs and she stepped out into a snow-blanketed Manhattan. The sun hadn't yet risen but everything from the sky to the ground was white. It would have been the most magical of sights if the wind hadn't whipped the thickly falling snowflakes straight into her face.

Cursing her demanding boss, Victoria tightened her coat's hood, hunched over, and set off on the three-block walk to Marcello's. Hopefully a cab would pass any mo-ment for her to hail.

It felt strange walking the streets virtually alone. New York was the city that never slept but this early morning, there was hardly any traffic on the roads and even fewer pedestrians. If she hadn't been a lady on a mission to get to her boss's apartment as quickly as possible, make his blasted coffee, and then get back to her own apartment before the storm really took hold, she'd be creeped out at the vulnerable state she, a young woman walking the streets with hardly anyone about, was in. At least there was plenty of light, and she took comfort too that any predators were likely to get one blast of the wind chill and slam their front door on it.

One block to go and a gust of wind nearly knocked her off her feet. The snow was now coming so thick and fast she could hardly see more than a few feet in front of her. Not that she could really see with the flakes all making a beeline for the exposed parts of her face.

To cheer herself up and make the final block bearable, she imagined maiming Marcello again. Nothing that would incapacitate him, she wasn't evil, just a minor breakage of, say, both his hands, a minor injury that would prevent him using his phone. And while she was at it, maybe a nice dose of laryngitis for him too, so he'd be prevented from speaking until she'd caught up with all the sleep eighteen months working as his executive assistant had deprived her of.

By the time she reached the towering art deco building, Victoria could no longer feel her nose, toes or the tips of her fingers. She had a dreadful feeling the overenthusiastic forecasters predicting the storm of the century were going to be proved right. She should have known it would be so when they'd named the storm Brigit. Her grandmother was called Brigit and she was the most cantankerous woman to grace God's earth.

When the rest of Victoria's family had reacted with stunned silence at her getting into Columbia in New York to study business, Grandma Brigit's immediate response had been to predict that Victoria would 'get shot because they all have guns there', and then demanded to know what was wrong with Ireland's universities. When the rest of Victoria's family had reacted with the same stunned silence at her being personally headhunted by a billionaire Italian businessman and investor, whose penchant for glamorous girlfriends saw him written about in the press's gossip columns with the same frequency as the business pages, Grandma Brigit's sharp nose had risen. 'Just you wait, girl,' she'd warned. 'He'll have you running rings for him. You'll be nothing but a glorified dogsbody.'

Victoria frequently thought that Grandma Brigit hadn't been wrong.

Still, for all Grandma Brigit's cantankerousness, she was the only member of Victoria's family who'd not been surprised at either Columbia or the headhunting, mainly because she was the only family member for whom Victoria wasn't a blurred face in the background.

Someone had gritted the building's main entry steps, and when she entered the lobby, its warmth was so welcome that she took a moment to savour it.

The on-duty concierge, who had a slightly frazzled demeanour that early morning, called Marcello's private elevator down while Victoria stamped snow off her boots. Inside the elevator, she pulled her gloves off and used her thumbprint to get it moving. No thumbprint or passcode, no entry into Marcello's private domain. The passcode was changed daily. Christina and Patrick, the currently incapacitated live-in staff, were the only people other than Victoria to have unquestioning access to the Manhattan apartment. Victoria was the only one to have unquestioning access to all Marcello's homes. Even his girlfriends had to make do with the ever-changing passcodes.

She remembered her pride when her thumbprint had been taken. The novelty had worn off by the end of the first month, when he'd woken her to request she arrange the immediate delivery of a crate of champagne. Not just arrange the delivery but supervise its unloading in the apartment. It had been one a.m. Delivery unloaded, she'd politely declined his offer to join the raucous party he'd been hosting. Five hours after she'd left his apartment, she'd arrived at the Guardiola Group's offices and found Marcello at his desk, looking as fresh as a daisy and in his usual upbeat, positive mood.

She stepped out of the elevator leaving a puddle of melted snow on its carpet.

It came as no surprise to find Marcello waiting for her in his reception room—he'd probably watched her through the elevator's security camera—or that he greeted her with, 'Did you get lost?' The only surprise was the stubble on his face. It was rare to see her immaculately groomed boss anything less than immaculately groomed. Sunday morning and he was half dressed for the office. All he needed was to shave, don his tie, waistcoat and suit jacket and he'd be good to step into any board meeting.

She arched an unimpressed eyebrow. 'Have you seen the weather?'

His expression was that of someone who didn't know what *weather* was. 'I have been waiting for you.'

'Well, I'm here now. I'll hang this lot up and then get your coffee made.'

'I need food too.'

Of course he did. Christina or Patrick usually fixed whatever he wanted for breakfast or arranged delivery. In the office, it was Victoria's job to ensure he never went hungry.

'What do you want?'

'Bagels.'

Wet clothes hung in the drying room by the reception, phone secure in the back pocket of her jeans, Victoria entered the vast loft space Marcello considered his home. Of all his properties, this was her favourite. It was just so quirky and interesting.

The main central room was the huge rectangular open-plan living space he hosted his sought-after parties in. Its exposed red brick was cut through with floor-to-ceiling leaded windows that let in an abundance of light and gave a panoramic view of Central Park. High ceilings accommodated galleried overhangs at each end. The overhang above the bottom end was the dining area used for dinner parties, a door off it leading to store rooms and the staff quarters where Christina and Patrick lived. The overhang above the other end was Marcello's home office. A door off the office led to the bedrooms, including his own, the only room Victoria didn't like going into. It wasn't that he'd ever made her feel unsafe or anything—on the contrary, she often got the impression he assumed she was an artificially constructed robot dressed in a woman's skin rather than an actual woman—it was more the feelings evoked when entering his most private domain, the strange queasiness at catching sight of the bed he slept in.

Long used to the magnificence of this most breathtaking bachelor pad, Victoria was too busy ordering bagels via the app of his preferred deli to pay it the slightest bit of attention. At the door under the dining room overhang, she turned her head and found her boss perched on the L-shaped sofa, dark brown leather like the rest of the plentiful seating, now engrossed in his phone.

'I'll show you how to fix the coffee in case Christina and Patrick are laid up for any length of time.'

He didn't look up from his phone. 'I am sure they will be better by tomorrow. Dr Jeffers said sleep is the best medicine for them.'

'You've had your doctor out?'

'He left just before I called you—he didn't know how to work the coffee machine.'

Only Marcello would have the nerve to call his private doctor out in the middle of the night and then expect him to prepare a pot of coffee for him.

Thawing slightly now she knew he'd had the decency to get medical attention for his two most devoted staff, she nonetheless knew to stand her ground. 'There's no guarantee they'll be better by tomorrow.' Manhattan, indeed the whole of New York, was currently plagued by a myriad of debilitating viruses. Marcello, though, was one of those infuriating people who never got ill and had little patience for those who did, expecting instantaneous recoveries from the inconveniently afflicted. 'Let me show you how to fix it for yourself in case you need it tomorrow.'

'I will call you if it becomes necessary.'

'It won't be necessary to call me if you learn to do it yourself.' Just as it wouldn't be necessary for him to call her when he fancied a late-night delivery of food if he'd bother installing the apps he'd insisted she install on *her* phone for the express purpose of ordering delicious goods for him in the hours he thought it unreasonable to wake his live-in staff.

It was the edge in Victoria's voice that made Marcello look up. Seeing the steel in her eyes, he gave a dramatic sigh. His executive assistant was superb at her job but there were times when she could be a little irritable. He forgave her those touchy episodes only because he didn't want to have to sack her. It wasn't the bother of finding a replacement that was at issue—Manhattan's streets were awash with highly efficient, highly qualified executive assistants—but the bother of having to train someone new. Besides, he liked Victoria's Irish accent. It was one of the reasons he'd poached her after his last assistant selfishly decided not to return after her maternity leave.

So, rather than point out that Victoria was paid generously in money and perks that included her own apartment to be on call whenever he needed her, he decided to humour her. After all, it *was* Sunday. 'Okay, show me how to fix the coffee.'

Marcello's kitchen was a room he only entered if looking for his staff. This was Christina and Patrick's domain, and the domain of the executive chefs he hired…well, who his staff hired on his behalf…when he was playing host. One of the many great things about New York was the abundance of staff for hire. For the right price, they would make themselves available whenever he needed, which meant he only needed two staff living in. Of course, Christina and Patrick hired regular workers to assist with the day-to-day chores but those were generally employed during office hours so he could enjoy his home undisturbed.

His specially imported precious coffee beans were kept in the fridge. It was the one thing he insisted on, a habit picked up from his childhood and his father's insistence that coffee beans remained fresher if kept refrigerated.

His own fridge was a huge triple American one that his mother had gaped in amazement at the first time she'd seen it. From it, Victoria removed the container of beans and carried them over to the coffee pot and placed them on the stainless-steel surface beside it.

Deciding to be a good boy, Marcello stood beside her and pretended to pay attention.

'Fill it with cold water up to the line,' she instructed

as she ran water into the pot. She was turning the tap off when her phone buzzed.

Sliding her hand into her back pocket, she read the message whilst carrying the pot back to the machine.

The short puff of air she expelled told him she'd just received unwelcome news.

She looked at him. She wasn't wearing any makeup, he noted. Not that she normally wore much of it but the little she did wear made its absence more noticeable now that he was looking at her face. She hadn't styled her dark red hair into the tidy ponytail she normally wore either. It was much longer than he'd thought, falling halfway down her back.

'The deli can't deliver.'

Assuming she was joking, he laughed.

Not smiling, she held her phone up so he could read the message for himself.

'Staff shortage due to inclement weather? What does that mean?'

'It means you should look out of a window.'

'I know *what* it means but what I want to know is why it should affect my bagel delivery. I am on the same block. Message back and tell them to get someone to walk it over.'

An eyebrow a browner shade than her hair arched. 'It says, quite clearly, that they don't have the staff.'

'Then call the concierge.'

A sharp rise and fall of her shoulders and then she did

as he asked whilst simultaneously adding coffee beans to the machine. It was a short conversation.

'The on-duty concierge is waiting for more staff to arrive,' she told him. 'They should be in a position to send someone out for you within the hour.'

That long? Marcello wanted his bagel now, not in an hour. What was wrong with the world that a bit of snow should cause such inconvenience?

'The coffee is prepared, it just needs to drip through,' she added. 'When the red light turns green, it will be ready to pour.'

'Great, then you can go and get me a bagel.'

The steel from earlier returned to her eyes. 'No, Marcello, now I go home.'

'But I am hungry. It will take you five minutes.'

'Ten in this weather. It's my day off and I've got plans.'

'If the weather is as bad as you keep whining about, your plans will have been cancelled.'

Her eyes widened. After a beat, she said, 'Whining?'

'Winter in Manhattan means bad weather,' he explained. 'You need to toughen up.'

While he waited patiently—and people thought he didn't have patience? Such a misconception!—for her to display some remorse and do as he'd requested, Victoria's now narrowed eyes did not leave his face. It was a long moment before he realised that mutiny rather than remorse had settled in them, a mutiny carried through to the lifting of her chin and the sucking in of her cheeks.

'I tell you what, why don't *you* toughen up? You're not an invalid. You've got a pair of fully functioning legs—if the weather out there's as tropical as you seem to think it is, then go and get your own damned bagel. I'm going home.'

To his astonishment, Victoria finished her tempered outburst by striding across the kitchen, her long red hair swishing behind her.

Incredulous, he took a few beats to realise she was being serious.

'Do I have to remind you the home you refer to comes courtesy of your job for me?' he called out.

'A job that this is my first day off from in eighteen days,' she retorted without looking back.

He strode after her. 'You think I take days off?'

She stepped through the door. 'I am your employee. I have a contract that affords me rights.'

The door almost closed in his face. Almost as put out at her failure to hold it open for him as he was by this bolshy attitude, which, even by Victoria's standards, went beyond minor insubordination, Marcello decided it was time to remind her who the actual boss was and of her obligations to him.

'You cannot say you were not warned of what the job entailed when you agreed to take it,' he said when he caught up with her in the living room. She was already at the door that would take her through to the reception room. 'It is why you are given such a handsome salary and generous perks.'

Instead of going through the door, she came to a stop and turned back round, folding her arms across her breasts. ‘Quite honestly, Marcello, the way I’m feeling right now, I’d give the whole lot up for one lie-in. One lousy lie-in. That’s all I wanted but you couldn’t even afford me that, could you? I tell you what, stuff your *handsome salary and generous perks*—I quit.’

Too astounded to do anything but laugh, he shook his head. ‘Now you are being…’

But she’d already disappeared into the reception room, again not holding the door for him. This one being a spring-loaded, reinforced safety door, he came within an inch of having his nose broken by it slamming on him.

His patience close to being fully evaporated, he pushed the door open and loudly said, ‘You have to give three months’ notice.’

She emerged from the drying room with her outdoor clothing bundled in her arms.

Poker-faced, she eyeballed him as she pressed her thumb to the pad that summoned the elevator. ‘Consider this my notice.’

‘Are you actively trying to put me off providing you a reference?’

She held her palm up beside her face and gave it a little wave. ‘Is this the face of concern?’

The elevator arrived.

‘If you leave now, I will sue you for breach of contract,’ he threatened.

Still not removing her gaze from his, she gave a defiant smile and stepped backwards into the elevator.

'I mean it, Victoria. I will sue you.'

Still smiling, she wound her scarf around her neck then, the doors closing, waved at him, this time in farewell. *'Ciao, amigo.'*

He wedged his foot in before the doors could fully close and slipped into the elevator with her. '*Amigo* is Spanish.'

'I know.'

'You can't quit over a bagel.'

She punched the button to get the elevator moving. 'I just did.'

'It is not valid until it is in writing.'

'I'll email HR as soon as I get home. Oh, and if you sue me, I'll countersue.'

'You have no grounds and you could not afford it.'

She rammed her woolly hat on her head, covering her ears. 'I think you'll find I can. My handsome salary and generous perks mean I've built quite the nest egg.'

'Then you do not want to lose it.'

'If I lose it, I go home and start again.'

He laughed. 'Home to Ireland? You love living in Manhattan. You would miss the nightlife.'

'My last night out was a date at the theatre. I made sure my boss knew I was going in the hope he'd leave me in peace for one night, and he still thought it acceptable to call me during the performance demanding I return to the office and help him find his Montblanc pen.'

The elevator had reached the ground floor.

Victoria walked out of it putting her coat on.

'The pen was a gift from my father and it was a request, not a demand,' Marcello defended himself as he kept step with her through the empty lobby.

'A request phrased as a demand.'

'You could have said no.' Ignoring the unimpressed face she threw at him, he added, 'You never did tell me who that date was with.'

'Someone who wasn't happy with me cutting and running on them for the sake of a pen.'

'But you are good at finding things.'

They'd reached the door that exited onto the street.

'And you're good at losing them.' Her hand reached for the door. '*Ciao*, Marcello.'

'Come on, Victoria, be reasona—'

A loud bang from outside made them both jump, and cut away Marcello's argument from his tongue.

'What the hell was that?' he muttered, darting to the nearest window.

The gentle fluttering of snow he'd risen to at his usual four a.m. had turned into a blizzard. He had to peer hard to make out the two cars that had collided right outside the entrance door.

CHAPTER TWO

THE SNOW WAS falling so hard that Victoria didn't realise Marcello had yanked open the driver's door of the first crunched-up car until she walked into him. Her apology dissolved into the howling wind.

The driver and sole occupant, a middle-aged man who looked dazed rather than injured, let them help him out.

'You take him inside,' she shouted at Marcello. The cold was biting through her thick winter clothing. Marcello didn't even have a suit jacket on to protect him. 'I'll see to the other car.'

'What?' he shouted back.

'Take him inside!'

She then shuffled through what had to be at least four inches of snow to the driver's side of the other car, and opened the door. The wind almost pulled it off its hinges.

Mercifully, there was only one occupant in this car too, a middle-aged woman who also looked more dazed than injured. Her airbag had been deployed and, after she'd fought her way out, she clung to Victoria, shouting an explanation as to why she was on the roads in such treacherous conditions that Victoria barely heard a word of. The wind was just too loud. Supporting the woman's weight, she guided her to the building. Incredibly, the woman was wearing a pair of stilettos, making the going slow and dangerous. Any moment and the woman would lose her footing and they'd both go tumbling. When Marcello emerged before them, she didn't know if she was horrified or grateful that he'd come back out.

'Anyone else?' he yelled close to her ear.

'No, this is it! Go back in! I've got her!'

Ignoring her, he lifted the woman into his arms and disappeared into the whiteness.

Virtually snow-blind, Victoria shuffled one foot in front of the other until she reached the steps. Clinging tightly to the railing, she made it to the top. Shoving the door open, she practically threw herself inside only to collide straight into rock-solid man.

An arm hooked around her back to steady her.

Blinking snow out of her eyes, she looked up and into Marcello's piecing blue stare.

The easy smile that was more familiar than any other spread over his face. 'I know you are cross about a bagel but do you have to keep slamming doors into me?'

His dryness collided with the surging relief that they were both inside and safe. It raced up her throat and expelled from her body as a short burst of laughter. The piercing blue eyes crinkled and then he burst into bemused, disbelieving laughter of his own.

After one quick squeeze of her waist and one dropped

kiss on the top of her snow-laden hat, he stepped away from her, shaking his head whilst running his hand through the melting snowflakes in his thick black hair.

Even though she knew intuitively that the squeeze and kiss were Marcello's own relief manifesting, it still made her blink. Marcello was very Italian in his mannerisms, very tactile…but never with her. Everyone who crossed the threshold into his office was greeted with a handshake and a kiss to each cheek. Victoria had sat in on countless interviews kicked off with the same greeting.

It was his charm, Victoria had long ago decided, that along with his smile disarmed people and stopped his tactile manner crossing into unwanted behaviour. It was part of the package that had made an ordinary Roman rise to the top and conquer Manhattan before his thirtieth birthday, when he finalised an audacious takeover of a multi-billion investment group. A strong work ethic, a body that required little sleep and an instinct about people that enabled him to spot a potential troublemaker or a latent genius within two minutes had been the other components in his rise.

Now aged thirty-six, he was the king of his own castle with a devoted workforce. Victoria doubted there were many workers in the Guardiola Group who wouldn't take a bullet for him. It was her own devotion that had held her back from resigning the fifty-odd times she'd considered it before. Because, as selfish and demanding as Marcello was, he was also generous and fun to be around. His bad moods were rare and always followed with an apology. He complained about Victoria's predecessor quitting but he'd been partly to blame for that by giving her an incredibly generous maternity package followed by an eye-watering bonus because, he'd confided with great, if misplaced, authority, 'Babies are not cheap to raise.'

That bonus had been the equivalent of two years' full salary.

When the woman in question, Denise, had brought the baby in for everyone to coo over, Victoria had not long started as her replacement. For all his complaints about Denise leaving him, Marcello had greeted her like a long-lost sister and spent so long cuddling and fussing the baby that the child probably left thinking he was his father. He didn't even complain when the baby brought up milky sick on his Armani suit.

And yet, for all his tactile ways, with Victoria, he was strictly hands off. For her birthday, he'd had their office decorated with balloons and banners, given her tickets to a Broadway show—her last full night off without him bothering her about something inane—she'd longed to watch but couldn't remember mentioning to him, and generally made a great big fuss of the day, all without giving her the smacking kisses to the cheeks everyone else received on their birthdays. The most he'd ever done was shake her hand when they'd got together to discuss the job he'd poached her for.

Shaking off the weird unsettling feeling his brief display of affection had provoked, she cast her attention to the drivers of the collided cars.

Quickly establishing they were both physically fine, she arranged for the concierge, who'd reappeared even more frazzled, to keep them fed and warm until the emergency services arrived, whenever that would be.

With nothing more to be done for them, Victoria rewound her scarf around her neck. 'You should go up and get some dry clothes on,' she advised Marcello. He had to be freezing after his Action Man heroics. If it was anyone else, she'd suggest a hot bath too.

His white shirt was drenched from the melted snow and she was having to make a concerted effort not to let her eyes dip down to the naked chest it now transparently covered. Dark hair that covered much of his ripped torso and brown nipples were clearly visible.

She'd only seen him topless once, around a year ago. Coffee in hand, they'd just left their office for the boardroom when an absent-minded tech guy had walked into him. Coffee had splattered all over his shirt.

Victoria's first boss, the one Marcello had poached her from, would have gone berserk and probably fired the tech guy on the spot. Marcello had reassured him the coffee was cold so no harm had been done, advised him to watch where he was walking in the future, then dived back into his office and through to the mini-dressing room at the far end where his emergency clothing was kept. Victoria had been checking her emails while waiting for him when he came out sticking his arms into a fresh shirt asking her something she'd long forgotten.

What she hadn't forgotten was the fuzzy sensation she'd experienced to see his bare chest. It was much the same sensation as when she imagined him asleep in his bed.

'So should you,' he told her.

'I will.' She set off to the door. 'Go and drink your coffee and get warm.'

'Where are you going?'

'Home,' she answered, surprised he'd asked.

He gave her the look he'd once given a trio of college leavers pitching for an investment in their start-up business of beer brewed with a twist. His expression when he'd actually tasted the beer had been such a picture that she'd barely held it together until they were finally alone and she could let it out. The two of them had laughed so hard tears had been streaming down their faces.

This look was the look given to the initial *We've decided to improve beer by adding strawberries to it* pitch: utter incredulity that someone should think of something so stupid.

'You are not.'

'You've experienced for yourself how bad it is out there and the storm's barely started. Imagine how much worse—'

'You are not walking home in that.' Marcello jabbed a finger in the direction of the window. 'It is too dangerous.' And there was not a chance in hell he would let Victoria step another foot in it.

'I'm not hanging around here waiting for it to pass. They're saying the storm could last a couple of days.'

'I don't care if they are predicting it to last for weeks. You're not going anywhere until it is safe.' He positioned his back against the door, barring her exit. 'You will stay with me.'

'Not necessary.'

He folded his arms across his chest. 'Completely necessary, and it is not an order dressed as a request but an order.'

'You're not my boss so you can't order me to do anything.'

'Your notice has not been given in an official capacity so I am still your boss, and as your boss I am ordering you to stay. You can endanger your life all you want once I have found a replacement for you,' he added.

The glare she threw at him was completely mitigated by the amusement dancing in her eyes and the twitching of her lips. 'Ah, so it isn't concern for me but concern for the management of your life.'

He smiled widely. 'Perfectly put.'

'They're saying everyone needs to stay at home,' the man they'd rescued called out to them. 'Only essential travel as of now. You should take the man up on his offer, lady.'

'See, *lady*?' Marcello said. '*They* agree with me. It is not safe for you to leave.'

She tilted her head and, her Irish lilt musing, said, 'How strange when barely an hour ago you thought it acceptable for me to go out in it and collect your bagel.'

'I wasn't to know the storm had come in so quickly, was I?'

'Of course not. After all, I only mentioned it a dozen times.'

'If I have told you once, I have told you a million times not to exaggerate.'

Her lips twitched again, her chin wobbling, a classic sign that Victoria was suppressing laughter.

Marcello had never met anyone with such similar humour to him before. He'd recognised it the day he'd met her, when she'd been the assistant of the CEO of a firm he'd been considering investing in. During the firm's presentation, anything that could have gone wrong had. Victoria had impressed him with her handling of it all, all grace under fire. It wasn't until the final slide that it had become apparent everything going wrong was due to sabotage. Instead of the usual boring variation of, *Thank you for your consideration* appearing on the screen, someone had replaced it with a still from an old popular musical film where three high school students flashed their bare backsides and 'mooned' to the camera.

The po-faced directors had been outraged. Marcello had thought it hilarious. One look at the curvy redhead's contorted face had only added to his delight. It was seeing the tortured suppression of her laughter that had made his own all the sweeter.

'Your staff must really hate you,' he'd observed once he'd stopped laughing. Then, unable to resist, he'd looked again at the redhead. She'd clamped her hand over her mouth. Her shoulders had been shaking. Tears had been in her eyes. Only the expression in them had betrayed her thoughts. Those eyes had clearly been telling him she couldn't hold it back much longer and implored him not to say another word.

He'd taken pity on her and declined the investment without any further quips.

When Denise had announced she wouldn't return from her maternity leave, he'd known exactly who to appoint as her permanent replacement, and it would be a cold day in hell before he let Victoria leave him…terminate her employment, he corrected himself. It would be a colder day in hell before he let her go back out into that storm.

Unfolding his arms, he held his hands up. 'Okay, I admit it. You were right and I was wrong, and as you were right you must see that walking three blocks in this weather is a suicide mission.'

Eyes narrowing, she lifted her chin. 'Do you take back the part where you accused me of whining?'

He sighed. '*Sì*, I take it back.'

Her eyes now widened as she eyeballed him and non-subtly cleared her throat.

He exaggerated the next sigh. 'I am sorry that I accused you of whining. Now, can we please go up to my apartment before I drop down dead of hypothermia?'

More lip twitching. 'I wouldn't worry about that—you carry enough hot air in you to keep your core temperature up longer than the rest of us mortals.'

He shook his head regretfully. 'More talk like that and I will have to sack you.'

Her twitching lips spread into a wide grin and she shook her head before heading to the elevator, loudly saying, 'You're an idiot.'

He clamped a hand to her shoulder as he fell into step with her. 'You love me really.'

He didn't even have to look at her to know she was rolling her eyes.

Maybe she had a point about him being full of hot air because the warmth in his chest as he rode his elevator back up to his apartment with his favourite person in the whole of New York was enough to take the edge off the chill of his skin.

With Marcello taking a hot shower to defrost, Victoria curled up on her favourite of his sofas with a mug of his precious and admittedly delicious coffee. She'd thrown her wet jeans in the tumble dryer—she would bet money he didn't know where it was located in his vast apartment—and been astounded to find them dry within minutes. Relieved too. No way did she want to be around Marcello with only tights and socks covering her legs. Her jumper barely skimmed her bum.

She turned the telly on. Storm Brigit and the destruction it was already causing dominated the news.

She flicked through the channels in the hope of finding a forecaster with a better prognosis for it. She'd settled on the most optimistic of them when she head Marcello's footsteps coming down the staircase that connected the ground floor to the overhang behind her.

He refilled his coffee from the pot she'd brought from the kitchen into the living room, and made himself comfortable on the L-shaped sofa to the side of the one she'd taken.

'Jeans?' she gasped with faux horror when she clocked he wasn't wearing a suit.

'Do not tell *Time* Magazine,' he quipped.

'They wouldn't believe me.'

He met her stare and grinned. Along with his faded blue jeans, he'd donned a long-sleeved black top that enhanced his muscular physique. Not that he was over muscly. He didn't aspire to be a bodybuilder or anything, but he liked to take care of himself and made regular use of the apartment building's humungous gym and swimming pool.

'Looks like we are going to be roommates for the next couple of days,' he said, nodding at the telly and the optimistic forecaster still trying to convince New York that the storm was predicted to blow itself out within forty-eight hours when all the other forecasters were predicting three days.

'Don't tell Jenna or she'll scratch my eyes out.' Jenna was Marcello's latest girlfriend. Victoria loathed her more than all the others.

'That's been over for some time,' Marcello admitted, allowing himself a quick side-eye to see her reaction.

'Oh, really?' She took a sip of her coffee. 'I'm sorry to hear that.'

'No, you're not.'

'You're right, I'm not.' Eyes glued to the television, she added, 'When did you end it?'

'The day I walked in on her speaking to you like you were something she had trodden on.' He'd been in one of the rare meetings he didn't need Victoria to accompany him to. He'd returned to the office suite he shared with her to find Jenna with her palms down on Victoria's desk sneering, 'You're just a no one secretary. It's pathetic.'

Her gaze whipped from the television to him. 'That was months ago.'

Three months to be exact. *'Sì.'*

'You never said.'

'It was not important.' He cast her another side-eye. 'You never thought to ask why I stopped scheduling dates with her?'

She fixed her gaze back on the weather report. 'Your romantic life is none of my business.'

'I would not call it romantic.'

'I don't want to know what you call it,' she said sweetly, then drained her coffee. 'Who are you dating now?'

'I thought it was none of your business?'

'It isn't. I'm just being nosy.'

He laughed. 'I am not dating anyone.' Hadn't dated anyone since Jenna.

Victoria faced him with fake alarm. 'Are you ill?'

He'd wondered that himself a few times in recent months. Since Marcello had moved to Manhattan a decade ago, in need of a fresh start and with a determination to put the pain of the past behind him, he'd been as relentless in his pursuit of women as with business, and every bit as successful. It helped that he'd arrived here having already accumulated a modicum of wealth and that he had a face and physique the opposite sex found attractive. It also helped that he wasn't looking for a wife so wasn't seeking a meeting of minds or any of that romantic stuff, which widened his dating pool considerably.

He'd done marriage. He'd done family. What he'd lost could never be replaced.

He knew he'd developed terrible taste in women and he didn't care. It was better that way. If he was to date someone like Victoria for example, someone he greatly respected, who shared the same humour and with whom he could hold an entire conversation without either of them opening their mouths, then it would not be so easy to just send a text message calling things off. Not so easy to remain unmoved and ignore the outraged replies. Dating someone like Victoria would be much less drama in the short term but messier in the long run.

And so he stuck to his wide dating pool filled with shallow beauties whose lives revolved around themselves. Or had because all the shallow beauties he'd met in recent months had left him cold. He could too easily imagine them speaking to Victoria in the same way Jenna had. He could tolerate all forms of behaviour if a warm body was guaranteed but he could not tolerate that.

He hauled himself up from the sofa. 'I am not ill but I *am* hungry.' Now that the drama from earlier was over and he was warm and dry again, his neglected empty stomach was demanding food. 'Would it be unreasonable to ask the agency to send a chef over?' he added tongue in cheek, referring to the agency Christina and Patrick employed the pool of domestic workers who worked their magic keeping his home clean and fresh. Top quality chefs were part of the agency's services.

'Yes,' she stated firmly.

He smiled.

Her eyes narrowed before, half laughing, she shook her head. 'I can't cook!'

'I will add an ever bigger bonus to your salary.'

'I meant it literally. I can't cook.'

'How can you not cook?'

'How can *you* not cook?'

'Because I employ people to do it for me.'

'I don't work for you.'

'You do until you have given and worked your notice.'

'I don't *have* to work my notice.'

'And I don't *have* to sue you for breach of contract.'

Victoria couldn't suppress a snigger. 'Seriously, the

only thing I can cook is toast. Oh, and instant noodles. Did you not learn your way around a kitchen before you become a spoilt billionaire?' He hadn't moved to Manhattan until he was twenty-six. His rise since his arrival had been stratospheric but she knew his background was modest and that he came from a family very similar to her own, but with fewer siblings and a less scary grandmother. She knew, too, from the grapevine, that he'd been married before his move to Manhattan, a short-lived marriage that's ending had left him devastated and swearing to never marry again. She'd often wondered what his wife had been like. Had she been an entitled bitch like his succession of lovers or someone normal? What did she have that no other woman had? What had gone so wrong between them that Marcello would become such an avowed bachelor?

All questions she would never learn the answer to. Marcello's marriage was the one subject that had never been discussed between them. As far as she was aware, he didn't even know that she knew he'd been married.

'I have managed to forget the few skills I learnt,' he informed her blithely.

'How convenient.'

'Being a spoilt billionaire is a very convenient excuse,' he agreed. 'What is yours?'

She smiled sweetly. 'Having a slave-driving, spoilt billionaire boss demanding my attention at all hours and leaving me reliant on take-out.'

CHAPTER THREE

VICTORIA STOOD IN Marcello's pantry struggling to keep her jaw from dropping open. This was one part of his apartment she'd never been in before, and *wow.* She had never seen so much food. It was like stepping into a condensed supermarket. The pantry itself was twice the size of her parents' kitchen.

'You could feed the whole of Manhattan with what's in here,' she commented, awed.

'Not quite,' he murmured, standing beside her.

'Close though. At least we won't starve. Can you see the eggs?'

They'd found packets of bacon in the fridge and agreed any idiot could cook that, then agreed that if any idiot could cook bacon, they could cook eggs too. When she'd asked where in the fridge said eggs were, he'd looked at her as if she really was an idiot.

She'd grinned. 'So you're not fully Americanised then?'

'I am afraid of my mother making a surprise visit,' he'd quipped. 'It is one of the few things of my childhood that has stuck with me. Coffee beans kept in the refrigerator, eggs kept at room temperature.'

Eggs and bread located, they went back into the kitchen. There was a lot of clattering and other noise as they searched the industrially equipped room equal in size to her full apartment for utensils and crockery.

Thirty minutes later and the immaculate kitchen looked like a chimpanzee's party had been hosted in it.

Sitting at the sprawling kitchen island, both looked dubiously at their plates of burnt toast, blackened bacon and rubbery scrambled eggs.

Despite her stomach rumbling whilst they'd been cooking, Victoria's appetite had disappeared and she could only manage half of hers. Marcello, though, ate every last scrap of his bar the pieces of cunningly hidden eggshell, then gazed longingly at her leftovers. She pushed her plate to him with a 'be my guest' gesture, and, feeling suddenly cold, rubbed her left arm for warmth. A mild pounding had formed in her head, and she drained her coffee hoping the caffeine would ease it.

When Marcello put his knife and fork together and slid off his stool, his body aimed at the door, Victoria folded her arms and glared at him. 'Don't even think about leaving me to clear this mess up.'

'The staff will do it when they come in.'

She rolled her eyes. 'There's not going to be any staff, Marcello, not with the stay-at-home mandate.'

His forehead furrowed and he rubbed his fingers through his thick black hair.

'It's a suicide mission to walk out there,' she added, reminding him of his own words.

She could see his clever brain thinking and was not in the least surprised when he said, 'I will double your salary for the month if you do it.'

'I've quit, remember?'

'You still have to work the notice you haven't given. Triple pay.'

'No.'

If she was going to be stuck in this apartment with him for the next few days then she would not allow herself to be bribed and charmed—suckered—into taking on the domestic chores. She would not allow herself to fall into any kind of domesticity with him, and it wasn't just because she hated housework. All five Cusack girls had been expected to muck in with household jobs. Victoria's job had been to wipe the place mats and clean the table. As she was the second youngest, her designated job had been the second easiest of the lot and still she'd loathed doing it, but she'd had to do it because with a family as large as the Cusacks, everyone was expected to muck in. Having a family as large as theirs meant she could have slipped away unnoticed by everyone except sharp-eyed Kara, the middle sister who would have sat on her if she'd sloped off. If Victoria had wanted to be a domestic goddess she'd have done like her second oldest sister, Mags, and cheerfully offered help with all the undesignated chores too, not hidden in her room and pretended to be deaf on the very rare occasion her parents remembered her existence enough to call her name.

Her main reason, though, was that Marcello would absolutely take advantage if she gave so much as an inch. It would start with cleaning the kitchen and end with him expecting her to do his laundry and pour all his drinks. After all, he hadn't started off as a total slave-driver when she'd first worked for him. He'd made unreasonable demands at all hours of the working week but initially her days off had been Marcello-free.

It had been over a year since she'd gone a whole day without at least talking to him. During her first Christmas in his employ, he'd called her twice during her week back in Ireland, and both calls had been necessary. The Christmas just gone, he'd called her every single day. In fairness, the call on Christmas Day itself had been to wish her a Merry Christmas from his family home in Rome.

It had been the strangest of calls, she remembered. There had been a melancholy in his voice, so faint that if she didn't know him so well she would never have detected it. By the time she'd gone to bed she'd been cursing his name for making her spend her favourite day of the year worrying about what the cause of the melancholy could have been. Their next conversation, the melancholy had been absent and in the two weeks since their return to normal working life, she'd been unable to bring herself to ask about it.

Not liking the reminder of how sick she'd felt for him

and the cause of his uncharacteristic melancholy, a reminder that increased the mild burning stabbing sensation in her head, Victoria pulled herself together and made an executive decision. 'You load the dishwasher and I'll clean the surfaces.'

He pulled his most unimpressed face.

She wasn't in the least perturbed. 'It's either that or we let the mess fester. I'll help but I'm not doing it on my own.'

'Quadruple pay.'

She rubbed her forehead with her palm to try and ease the burny stab. 'Quit the bribes and load the dishwasher.'

Marcello knew when he was beaten.

Giving a theatrical sigh, he picked up his plate. 'How do I do it?'

With a roll of her eyes…ouch, that hurt…she shook her head. 'You're the smartest man I know. You can work it out.'

His ego inflating at the compliment, Marcello went in search of the dishwasher, then watched a video on how to load it and hoped the end result would be better than the video on grilling bacon.

He tried to remember when he'd last performed a domestic chore. Certainly before his short marriage with Livia ended. When they first married, they'd earned enough between them to employ a weekly cleaner. By the time grief drove them apart, Marcello had earned enough on his own for a full-time housekeeper. His mother had half-heartedly tried to domesticate him as an adolescent but he'd been excellent at feigning uselessness at it, so much so that she decided it was easier to just continue doing the chores herself.

Victoria, he thought, watching her lean over to wipe the marble island, would never put up with that. She'd insist the adolescent keep practising until they mastered the art of running a vacuum cleaner around a room...

She stretched right over the island to reach a spot in the middle. Her sweater had risen and suddenly he had a full display of curvy bottom clad in tight jeans in his eyeline.

Much practice meant he was able to immediately avert his gaze and give his attention back to trying to figure out how to turn the damned dishwasher on.

Experience had taught him the slightly weightier beats of his heart would soon lighten.

He'd headhunted Victoria as Denise's replacement knowing intellectually that she was an attractive woman but never allowing himself to see her as such. There were occasions when he would observe her working on her computer or chatting on the phone or doing some other work-related task, and experience a wave of awareness. Other occasions, usually early mornings, when they shared the back of his car on the way to a meeting or an airport somewhere and she was still so fresh from the shower that he could smell her shampoo and the cleanliness of her skin, and have to block off his senses.

All those things were manageable. He made them manageable. Allowing himself to see her for the beautiful, curvaceously sexy woman she was would only lead to unwanted desires springing to life, which would then lead to a mess that would disrupt the efficiency of his life. And so he didn't allow it. Victoria was his executive assistant, his right-hand woman. She'd become indispensable to him.

'Here,' she said, her musical lilt breaking into his thoughts and the curvaceously sexy body he was trying to tune out breaking into his space to stand beside him and place the grill pan in front of him. 'You missed this.'

'How is that supposed to fit in it?'

'Let me check my guide to loading a dishwasher.'

He turned to face her.

She was staring at her opened palm. Shaking her head ruefully, she met his stare. 'I'm so sorry. The guide's not working. You'll have to figure it out all by yourself like a big boy.'

Ignoring her jest, he leaned his face more closely to hers. Was he imagining that she'd lost colour in her cheeks? Victoria was so naturally pale that it was hard to tell but there was something about her colour that made him ask, 'Are you feeling okay?'

She gave the slightest wince. 'Your whining has given me a headache.'

With any other woman he'd immediately come back with the quip used by men for what was probably millennia. Instead, he said, 'Do you need painkillers?'

'No need for you to take such drastic action on my behalf.'

He grinned. 'Go and sit down. I will finish up in here,' he added magnanimously.

Her eyes widened in alarm. 'Are *you* feeling okay?'

He only just restrained himself from giving her big, beautiful bottom an affectionate slap.

The snow was falling so thickly that Victoria could hardly make out any of Central Park. Manhattan was no longer blanketed in white. It was laden with it. Once the storm cleared, she'd get herself a sled and head to Pilgrim Hill.

One of her fondest childhood memories was of her family all trudging through foot-high snow to the nearest decent slope and sledging on bin bags for what had felt like hours. She'd sat on her mother's lap, she remembered, a treat that had been as rare as having enough snow to sledge on. She remembered, too, how she'd cried when her mother, deciding they were all in danger of turning into popsicles, had made the unilateral decision to return home. The promise of hot chocolate had dried Victoria's tears, and when they'd trooped through the front door and her mother had seen how blue the girls' fingers were, she'd whipped the youngest two, Victoria and Sinead, upstairs and run them a bath, staying to lift them out and dry them, another treat as rare as the snow. Mags had usually supervised Victoria's bath time.

It had been one of the best days of her life, and her already chilled body shivered in remembrance at how wonderfully cold it had been that day and yet how wonderfully warm she'd felt inside under the glow of her mother's attention.

Her brain, though, was still burning, and she pressed

her forehead to the cold window pane and dimly wondered if Marcello would like to go sledging with her. As quickly as she thought it, she discarded it. Sheena, her old roommate, would definitely be up for it. That was if she'd forgiven Victoria for abandoning her at the theatre for the sake of a missing Montblanc pen.

Her head was really hurting. And she was still shivering. Marcello's usually tropically heated apartment felt like an igloo.

She was about to climb off the windowsill she'd sat herself on and go to find him for some of the painkillers he'd suggested just fifteen short minutes ago, when he finally came out of the kitchen. Even with her suddenly fuzzy vision, Victoria could see his top was soaked.

'What happened?' Her voice sounded as fuzzy to her ears as Marcello was to her eyes.

'The dishwasher is faulty.'

'How?'

'It made banging noises after I turned it on so I opened it. The top thing that spins around and sprays water was hitting the grill thing.'

That explained why he was wet. From the look on his fuzzy face, Victoria was clearly at fault for not pointing out the danger of this happening.

She scrambled for a quip but nothing came to her. It wasn't just her sight and hearing that had become fuzzy but the whole of her goosebump-flecked body. Her burning brain had become incapable of conjuring even a minor jest.

Marcello, anticipating a witty retort, was disconcerted when nothing came. Surely she must have a riposte for him? 'Is your head still hurting?'

Her answering nod was small, as if it hurt to make too much movement.

Disconcertment turned into concern. Victoria had been his assistant for eighteen months. They worked so closely together that he'd learned to recognise the signs of her cycle, knew that when she spent a couple of days being a touch irritable, in another week she would silently suffer the stomach cramps that had her bring a hot-water bottle to the office and hold it to her abdomen whenever she thought he wasn't paying attention. He wouldn't dream of embarrassing her by asking if she needed anything in those times, but this was different. His brave, stoical executive assistant, who'd never taken a single day off sick, had pain etched on her face.

'You should lie down.'

His concern deepened when, instead of arguing, she gave another small nod.

Concern turned to alarm when she slid off the windowsill and her knees buckled. He had no doubt that if she hadn't gripped the armchair to the side of the sill, she would have collapsed onto the floor.

He strode straight to her.

'I'm fine,' Victoria whispered, holding a palm out to stop Marcello's blurry figure getting any closer. 'Just got a bit dizzy.'

She blinked rapidly to clear her vision but each blink

hurt her eyes and hurtled sharp pins into her burning brain. In the deep recesses of her mind was the knowledge that she'd caught one of the viruses debilitating New York, likely the one that had incapacitated Patrick and Christina overnight. She needed to lie down. Needed to get warm.

All she could allow herself to focus on was the long sofa. It was four steps away at the most.

Aware—much too aware—of Marcello standing to her side watching her, aware of his apparent concern, she took the first step, silently begging her legs to keep the rest of her upright. Of all the people in all the world to fall ill in front of, Marcello was the absolute worst.

Fighting through the swimming sensation that had now added itself to the burn in her brain, using legs that seemed to have become detached from the rest of her body, she took the next step…

The room began to spin.

'Victoria?'

She swayed.

The spinning sped up.

His next call of her name came like a distant echo in her ear as the whole world spun around her and then turned to grey.

Marcello caught her mid-fall. Hooking an arm around her waist, he tried to help her stand but Victoria's legs weren't cooperating. With his only other option being dragging her to the sofa, he lifted her into his arms like an injured child and cradled her to his chest.

Her eyes flew open. 'What you doing?' she mumbled.

'Getting you to a bed,' he decided firmly. That was where she needed to be. In bed. He knew because that was what the doctor had said when he'd called him out after Christina and Patrick had been struck down. Christina had deteriorated as quickly as Victoria. Sleep, the doctor had decreed, was the best medicine.

'No,' she protested weakly even as her cheek flopped against his neck. *Dio*, he could feel the elevated heat of her skin. She was burning up.

'Do not argue,' he scolded, heading for the stairs. 'You are not well.'

'Too heavy.'

Tuning out that her breath was hot against his skin and that her breasts were pressed against his chest, he lightly said, 'What did I just say about not arguing?'

Perfectly buxom though Victoria was, she was by no means too heavy for him to carry up the open stairs like a superhero. Through his office he took her and into his sleeping quarters, where he made a split-second decision and carried her into the closest room, which just happened to be his own. It had the most comfortable mattress and, unlike the guest rooms, had a sofa long enough for his six-foot-two body to sprawl out on while watching over her.

The curtains were still drawn, the duvet still thrown back from when he'd got up that morning, his incapacitated staff being unable to open the curtains or provide him with the freshly laundered bedding he enjoyed daily. She made hardly any movement as he carefully laid her down, her only word, 'Cold.'

'You are cold?' he clarified, gingerly resting his hand on her burning forehead. Now that she was lying down, there was no need for further physical contact.

'Cold,' she repeated, barely audible, slowly drawing her legs to her chest. Her eyes were closed.

He scratched the back of his head, unsure what to do. Did you put a duvet around someone with a fever? Reasoning she could always throw it off if she overheated, he covered her before stepping back to congratulate himself on a job well done. Superhero that he was, he'd saved his assistant from hurting herself in a faint and selflessly carried her into his own bed. He would remind her of this the next time she implied he was selfish.

'I will get you painkillers,' he said, keen to add more gold stars to his name on the off chance that she really was considering leaving him…quitting her job.

Her, ''K…' came out like a sigh.

This, though, posed its own challenge as, for all his talk about painkillers, Marcello didn't actually possess any. Not wanting to disturb his stricken housekeeper and butler, who must surely have a stash of the stuff, he put a call through to the concierge. It took ten whole minutes for a small tub of ordinary painkillers to be sent up to him in his elevator.

Armed with a glass of water and the means to ease Victoria's temperature and pains, he returned to his bedroom.

She was huddled in the sheets on her side, only the top of her head poking through.

To wake her or not to wake her? That was the question. Crouching down, he lightly pressed his fingers to the inch of exposed forehead. He squeezed his eyes tight and breathed hard. Too hot. Much too hot.

'Victoria?' he whispered loudly. 'You need to wake up and take some painkillers.'

Her eyes didn't open. 'Head hurts,' she mumbled.

'I know. This will make you feel better.'

'Can't.'

'Can't what?'

'Move. Hurts.'

'You want me to help you?'

She made the smallest nod even as she gave a nearly audible, 'No.'

Chuckling softly, he removed two of the tablets from the tub, placed them by the glass, then sat himself beside Victoria and carefully slipped an arm beneath her. 'I am just going to lift you a little so you can take your pills,' he told her.

She gave no protest, verbal or otherwise.

It took only a little effort to raise her so she was semi-upright. Holding her securely to him with his right arm, he reached for the water and pills with his left.

'Open your mouth,' he commanded.

She obeyed. He placed a tablet on her tongue without making any direct contact, then held the glass to her lips. Her hair tickled his throat and chin as she took the water into her mouth and swallowed.

'One more.'

Her lips parted again. This time his precision failed him and his finger brushed against soft, plump bottom lip then soft, plump, wet tongue.

Marcello's chest and airwaves tightened. His grip on the glass when he held it to her mouth a second time was much firmer than his first, reflexively gripping harder still when her hand fluttered up and tentatively covered his in silent encouragement for him to feed her more water.

He didn't know if it was her fever causing it but his own skin heated. The core temperature she'd teased him about only hours ago rose.

It felt like time stood still while he waited for the signal that she'd had enough, a passage of time where, in an effort to disassociate himself from the soft body leaning against his and the slender hand covering his own, he conjured images of dancing nuns and didn't dare to breathe.

Her hand flopped away from his.

He expelled the breath he'd been holding. 'Done?'

Another tickle of her hair as she nodded and whispered, 'Thank you.'

Putting the glass back on the bedside table, he carefully extricated himself from his role of human support and, doing his utmost to touch her as little as humanly possible, helped her lie back down.

She turned her cheek onto the pillow and gave a tiny whimper.

It was a sound that pierced through him.

A second whimper had him closing his eyes and forcing air into his lungs as he was carried back to the darkest days of his life, a time of unbearable loss and a grief so debilitating he could hardly breathe through it.

CHAPTER FOUR

CHANGED INTO A T-shirt and pair of pyjama bottoms gifted by his brother as a joke birthday present, and which he'd never worn before as he always slept nude, Marcello quietly padded into his room carrying a bundle of bedding taken from a guest bed. Outside, the storm continued to wage its war on the East Coast. The news was reporting half of New York being without power. Guessing it was only a matter of time before his apartment was similarly affected, he'd dug out the scented candles his mother gifted him each year under the delusion they would add a feminine touch to the apartment he'd determined before he'd even bought it would remain a bachelor pad for the rest of his existence.

For the first time in a long time, Marcello thought back to the home he and Livia had created together and the room they'd turned into a nursery. They'd spent hours searching for the best furniture to fill it with, and the best wallpaper and curtains to cover its walls and window. Giraffes. That had been the theme they'd chosen. Cute, cartoon-like giraffes that bore no resemblance to the real-life versions but were close enough that he still couldn't bear to see a giraffe in any shape or form. After moving to Manhattan, he'd deliberately avoided Central Park Zoo until discovering by chance that they didn't house them.

Pushing the memories away, he gave his attention back to the person who needed it most.

The insulation in his bachelor pad was so good that no sound of the raging storm penetrated. In his bed, though, lay Victoria, fighting her own personal storm. He had no thermometer and the concierge service had been unable to assist, so he had only his hands to judge that her temperature was worsening. Had only his eyes to see her struggle to keep warm one moment then to cool down the next.

Once he'd made a bed for himself on the sofa, he braced himself and went back to her with more painkillers. If he could have given them to her an hour ago he would have but Dr Internet—his own doctor wasn't answering his calls—had been firm that this brand and dose of painkillers could only be taken every six hours. This would be the third lot he'd fed her. She'd been a dead weight in his arms for the second batch, unable to support her own head. He supposed it was some inherent survival instinct that had enabled her to take the water into her mouth to wash the tablets down, and it was the one thing that kept the coldness of fear in his heart at bay and enabled him to leave her for a few minutes at a time.

Gently lifting her upright, his heart stuttered to find

her hair wet and plastered to her skull and her sweater drenched. The sheet beneath her was soaked with her perspiration. Fever almost crackled on her skin.

The cold fear broke free and grabbed at his throat.

He took a long breath. Parked the fear. Forced himself to think logically. Panicking did not help anyone. He'd learned that the hard way.

First things first. Painkillers and water.

As docile as a newborn lamb, she let him feed them to her.

Clenching his jaw, he breathed in deeply then said, 'Victoria, you need to take your sweater off.' And everything else. He didn't need Dr Internet to tell him she was overheating.

There was the slightest movement of her head against the crook of his neck.

'Can you lift your arms for me?'

She could barely raise her hands to her elbows.

There was nothing else for it. He would have to do it himself.

'We need to cool you down,' he said in what he hoped was a conversational tone as he manipulated her arms out of the sweater's sleeves whilst keeping her secure against him. 'Lift your head for me.' Her feeble attempt at this fortified him. Somewhere in Victoria's delirious mind she knew he was helping her and was trying to express her consent.

Refusing to let his mind return to the last time he'd held another helpless, overheating human being, he kept a tight hold of her burning body and used his left hand to pull the sweater over her head.

Although he knew to expect it, it still made his chest sharpen to find her fevered skin drenched with perspiration. Her soaked vest top clung to her.

Don't debate it, just do it, he told himself firmly. A minute later, the vest was off and discarded with the sweater. A quick pinch of the fastenings and a skim down her arms and her wet bra was removed too. He didn't even look at it as he threw it on the pile.

Manoeuvring her to the other, dry side, of the bed, resolutely refusing to acknowledge the weighty bare breast pressed against his biceps, he laid her back down, then quickly pulled off his T-shirt and covered her torso with it to protect both her modesty and his eyes.

'Nearly there,' he said. 'Just your jeans now.'

She mumbled something. A hand fluttered to the button and groped ineffectually at it before flopping back to her side.

'It is okay, I've got this,' he assured her.

Mindset fixed on the job in hand, Marcello unbuttoned the jeans, pulled the zip down then tugged at them. He couldn't get them or the tights—tights? Was wearing tights beneath jeans even a thing?—past her hips. 'See, now you know why I work out,' he told her as he slid a hand under her bottom and lifted it so he could ease the jeans and tights down to her thighs. 'It is in case a member of my staff is incapacitated by a virus and needs my superhero strength to undress them.'

He needed to keep talking, for both their sakes, and as he pulled the damp jeans and wet tights down her legs, using every ounce of his resolve not to look at the scrap of black cotton covering her pubis, the one item of clothing he would not under any circumstances touch, he kept the chatter going. He hoped like hell that she could hear him and was comforted and reassured by it.

Her jeans became stuck at the ankles, preventing him pulling them or the tights over her feet. Damn it, she was wearing socks over the tights! No wonder she was burning like a furnace.

A minute of intense concentration later and the jeans, tights and socks were all removed.

'I am going to get you…'

His intention of telling her he was going to get a cold cloth to wipe her face died on his tongue.

While he'd been removing the last of Victoria's clothing, she'd pulled the T-shirt off her chest. Unprepared, he had nothing to stop his gaze filling with her semi-naked form. Nothing to stop the curvaceous body he'd spent eighteen months pretending was as ordinary as any other body from soaking straight into his retinas.

Victoria opened her eyes. Sharp pain filled them. Her room was in darkness.

Not her room, she remembered through the pneumatic drill pounding in her head. One of Marcello's guest rooms.

She'd dreamed she was in Dante's *Inferno*.

She needed to use the bathroom. She reached through her befuddled brain for where it was. All the rooms in the apartment had an en suite, all situated on the opposite side of the room to the bed. She tried to sit up. A pain lanced her head, so sharp she cried out and flumped back onto her pillow.

'Victoria?'

Marcello?

She heard sheets rustling and then a shape emerged before her. Fingers pressed against her forehead.

She could hardly move her mouth to weakly ask, 'What are you doing?'

'Checking your temperature,' he answered quietly. 'I think your fever has broken.'

'What?'

'That is what Dr Internet calls it. It means the worst is over.'

'My head hurts.' Hurt so much. Everything hurt.

'I am sorry. You need to wait another hour before you can take more painkillers.'

A tear rolled down her cheek. She needed the bathroom but didn't think she had the strength to make it there.

'I need…' Her mouth was too parched to get any more words out.

'The bathroom?' he guessed.

She gave the weakest nod she could physically endure.

A dim light came on, as if he knew brightness would hurt her eyes.

The strange fog she'd been caught in for so long she didn't know if hours or days or weeks had passed reclaimed her. In an almost dreamlike state, she let Marcello lift her into his arms.

A strong sense of comfort in the sureness of his steps and the protective way he cradled her allowed Victoria to close her eyes and relax into him.

Faint light pouring in from the opened blind of the window drenched the dark bathroom in a faint glow.

'Can you take it from here?' he asked as he gently put her on her feet but kept hold of her so she had his strength as support.

Even through the heavy fog and dim memory of Marcello saving her from Dante's *Inferno* by stripping her clothes off her…she had no recollection of him putting the T-shirt she was wearing on her…there was a recoiling of horror at the thought of him watching her use the bathroom. 'Yes.'

He nodded. 'I will be right on the other side of the door.'

She wanted to tell him not to listen but the words wouldn't form.

He smiled, reading her thoughts again. 'I promise to close my ears. Now put your hand on the sink for support.'

Outside the closed bathroom door, Marcello rolled his neck, closed his eyes and concentrated on breathing. It wasn't enough to stop images of Victoria from dancing behind his lids.

It had taken more strength than he'd known he possessed to cool her face with a wet cloth and pat her dry with a towel, superhuman strength to remain dispassionate whilst manipulating her unresponsive body into the T-shirt. Of all the things he'd done for her, that had been the hardest, only the knowledge that she would be deeply embarrassed to wake virtually naked with him in the room spurring him on. When she came back to herself, she would be embarrassed enough to remember what he'd had to do for her.

The faint sound of fingers tapping the bathroom door had his eyes snap open and his chest swell. Opening the door a fraction, he spoke through the crack. 'Are you done?'

Fingers appeared through the crack in answer and gripped the frame surrounding the door.

He opened the door slowly, afraid of knocking it into her too-weak body…had it really been less than a day since she'd taken delight in slamming doors on him?

She was pressed against the wall to the side of the door, her cheek resting against the cool tile. He didn't know if it was a trick of the snow-white light seeping into the room but she was deathly pale.

Dio, even looking as wretched as it was possible for a human to look, she was beautiful.

'Let's get you back to bed,' he said as he cloaked himself with more much needed dispassion and hooked an arm around her. Carefully manoeuvring her so she leaned into him, he added, 'Can you walk?'

Her head rubbed against his shoulder in a nod.

'Hold onto me.'

Fingers slid slowly across the back of his waist then curved to a rest around his hip. Her temperature had dropped considerably since those frightening witching hours yet the burn of her touch cut through the cotton of his pyjama bottoms and seeped into his skin.

Breathing heavily, doing everything he could to block the sensations alive in him, Marcello steered Victoria to the bed and helped her into it, lifting her legs when she didn't have the strength to lift them herself.

'Duvet on?'

The tiniest of nods.

He covered her in it. 'Go back to sleep. I will wake you when it is time for more painkillers.'

When he was about to step away, her eyes fluttered open and locked onto his. A hand poked out of the duvet and stretched to him. He took hold of it. She gave his fingers the lightest of squeezes before giving the deepest sigh and falling back into sleep.

The first thing Victoria registered was that the pneumatic drill in her head had dimmed to a dull ache. Opening her eyes, she registered that she wasn't in a guest room but in Marcello's bedroom. The guest rooms, though spacious, were smaller, and decorated luxuriously but neutrally. Marcello's room by contrast was huge, and had deep grey panelled walls with splashes of deep, rich colour in the artwork and plentiful soft furnishings. She'd always imagined he'd hired an interior decorator and told them to create the most masculine bedroom possible so as to repel any woman from thinking she could stay more than a night in it.

How many nights had she slept in here? One? Two? Time had slipped away from her. The curtains were open on the floor-to-ceiling window her eyes had opened to, the light diffusing through the thick snow still falling telling her daytime was slipping away.

Bracing herself for pain, she lifted her head. The pain was enough to make her wince but nothing as bad as what she'd suffered before.

The worst really was over. Or had she imagined Marcello saying that?

And there he was, sprawled out on the leather sofa at the far wall opposite the bed, phone in hand, an arm hooked behind his head, hooked-together ankles and bare feet dangling off the end. A heap of bedding had been dumped on the floor beside him.

Blurry memories played like snapshots before her eyes and a swelling like she'd never experienced before released in her chest, gratitude and something indefinable filling her and rising up her throat with force enough to stop her calling out to him.

To see him lying there in…pyjama bottoms? Marcello was wearing pyjama bottoms? She would never have imagined that…and plain black T-shirt, ungroomed thick black hair mussed and sticking out in all directions, strong jaw covered in thick black stubble…

He must have sensed her stare for he turned his face.

Their eyes locked. After a long beat, the smile that had caused a thousand women's hearts to break lit his face. Laughter lines crinkled the corners of his eyes and for the very first time Victoria was unable to stop herself from seeing exactly what it was that other women saw when they looked at Marcello Guardiola.

The swelling in her chest crushed against her ribs.

'How are you feeling?' he asked, swinging his long legs to the floor.

It took a long time before she was able to answer. 'Better.'

'You look better,' he said approvingly. 'I have been worried about you.'

She couldn't take her eyes from him. All the things about him that she'd steadfastly refused to see on anything but a superficial level were right there before her, and she was helpless to stop herself drinking in every inch of the ruggedly handsome face and the hard, lean body he'd used as a pillar and shield to stop her falling.

'Hungry?'

She shook her head, unable to speak through the pulses suddenly raging in her throat.

'Not even for soup?'

Why couldn't she drag her gaze from him?

'I will make you chicken soup,' he decided at her non-answer. 'Dr Internet and my mother—she sends you her best wishes—say it is the best thing for you. If you can't manage it, I will eat it.' He looked at his watch. 'You can have more pain relief soon too.' He rose to his feet and stretched. His T-shirt rose, exposing the flat of his abdomen and the swirls of dark hair around his navel. 'There is water on your bedside table. Do you need my help to drink or need me for anything else before I go downstairs?'

The beats of her heart were racing like a drum in her ears. She gave another shake of her head.

He leaned over to the round table at the head of the sofa, picked up her phone and placed it on the bedside table. 'If you are feeling up to it, you should call your family.'

She stared at him blankly.

'They called to see you were keeping safe from the storm,' he explained.

Did they? she wondered dimly as her gaze remained glued to Marcello's ruggedly handsome face.

'I had to tell them you were ill,' he continued. 'I do not think they are convinced I have been looking after you well, so if you do speak to them, make sure to tell them my skills as a nurse are as exceptional as my skills in business. And please, assure your grandmother that I have not locked you in a basement.' His left eyebrow rose then wriggled. 'Does she breathe fire?'

Not waiting for an answer, he strode out of the room leaving Victoria staring at his retreating figure with the terrifying sensation that she'd caught a secondary virus.

It took more effort to use her hands than she'd have believed possible but somehow Victoria managed to post on the Cusack family messaging group, assuring them she was over the worst of her illness. Marcello must have laid her illness on thick to get them worried. She'd once woken with the most horrendous period cramps, so bad she'd been unable to haul herself out of bed for school, and no one had noticed her failure to make it down to breakfast. The first her parents knew she was still in bed had been via an alert from the school telling them she'd failed to arrive there. Her mum had called the house to see why Victoria hadn't gone to school, then told her to take some painkillers. She hadn't deemed period cramps worthy of popping home in her lunch break to check on her fourth youngest daughter.

Looking back, Victoria understood her mother's blasé attitude—she'd been through it already with the three older girls—but for Victoria, frightened and in pain, her indifference had hurt.

Grandma Brigit immediately responded to her message, and demanded proof it was Victoria who'd written it and not 'that man', which brought the kernel of a smile to her face. Knowing she would otherwise be bombarded with demands of proof in perpetuity, she took a selfie of her face on the pillow and winced at the image taken. Not having the energy to retake it, she pressed send and then used the last of her reserves to delete the image from her files.

She didn't even have the energy to stop herself from thinking about Marcello.

As sleep wound its tentacles back around her, she

soothed herself that the swell of feelings for him had been simple gratitude for the simple fact that he'd been her saviour. He'd stepped up when she'd needed him—the first time she'd ever needed him—and got her through the worst illness of her life. That it had felt more than heartfelt gratitude was a mirage caused by her defences being low and her frazzled mind playing tricks on her.

She was sinking back into sleep when the man whose face was lodged behind her closed eyes returned to the room.

Her heart kicked before her eyes opened.

'I bring soup,' he said proudly. He placed a tray on the table by the armchair at the side of the bed, then sat on the edge of the bed beside her. 'You are going to try and eat?'

The look in his eyes…had they always been such a clear shade of blue?…told her that this was a question with only one possible answer. Marcello was determined she should have some sustenance.

See, she assured herself. This was why her heart was racing: a manifestation of her gratitude.

She remembered how her heart had skipped all those many months ago. She hadn't recognised the number flashing on her ringing phone and had braced herself for a scam call. When Marcello had announced himself and then announced why he was calling, her heart had skipped and then raced so hard she'd taken an age to respond. So long had her silence gone on that he'd assumed she wasn't interested and increased the salary offer he'd just made by fifty thousand dollars. He didn't know she'd been too gobsmacked to answer.

She'd remembered him—of *course* she'd remembered him—but it had never occurred to her that he'd remembered her too. That this business titan had remembered her, remembered because he'd *seen* something in her, and gone out of his way to track down her personal number and offer her a job…

For the woman who'd grown up lost in the midst of siblings who all shone brighter than her…

She still didn't know which had meant the most to her, the remembering or the job offer, but, as demanding a boss as Marcello could be, she'd never forgotten how that one call had made her feel. Seen. Special. Things she'd never felt before.

And now, on top of all the care he'd given her, he'd made her soup.

She'd never gone so long without eating before and though she wasn't hungry, she knew she should at least try.

For the first time since she'd fallen ill, she was entirely aware of the muscular strength of Marcello's arm when he slid it beneath her, and wholly aware of the warmth of his hard body when he helped her sit up by resting her against him. Still holding her securely, he leaned over to grab some pillows. In an instant, her senses filled with the scent of faded cologne and warm skin.

She didn't know relief could feel like dejection when, finally satisfied that she was suitably propped up and unlikely to flop back down, he moved away from her. She didn't know, either, if she was imagining how quickly he released his hold on her and got off the bed, or if she was imagining that he spent a long time at the tray before carrying a large steaming mug to her. She didn't know, either, if it was the heat of the mug or the heat of his fingers making sure her hands were wrapped securely around the mug that sent warm sensation through her hands and into her bloodstream.

'You must eat all of it—I made it myself,' he said lightly.

She cleared her throat and tried to convince herself that her racing pulses were due to the virus. 'Really?'

'*Sì*. I have put it in a mug for you so you will find it easier to manage than with a bowl and spoon.' The smile that contained equal dollops of mischief and sexiness flashed at her. 'It would have been ready sooner but I could not find a tin opener.'

Marcello could hardly credit the strength of his relief to see a real smile form on Victoria's pale face at this, and see amusement spark in her eyes.

For the first time he allowed himself to admit that there had been moments during the long night when he'd feared he would never see her smile again. It had been the longest, most frightening night he'd experienced in eleven years.

Moving the armchair to within a foot of the bed so

he was close to hand if she needed him, he parked himself on it and was filled with even more relief when she sipped her way through all the soup. By the time he took the empty mug from her, a hint of her old colour had returned to her cheeks. He didn't kid himself that she was magically better but these little things meant she'd taken the first steps on her road to recovery. They meant that, tonight, he could sleep with his eyes and ears closed.

'You have called your family?' he asked.

She shook her head tiredly. 'I messaged the family group.'

'Good. Put their minds at rest.' He'd only answered her phone because *Mam* had flashed on the screen when it rang. His own mother kept calling too, as he'd stupidly let slip that he'd gained a house guest who'd fallen ill. She seemed as unconvinced as the Cusacks that he was taking proper care of Victoria. 'They have been calling every hour—they are worried about you.'

Her smile was as tired as her head shake. 'You must have told them I was dying.'

That took him aback. 'Why do you say that?'

'They're not ones for making a fuss.'

Seeing she was in no state to argue, he held off from commenting that if that was the Cusacks' definition of not making a fuss, he would hate to see what a real fuss consisted of. 'I told them only that you had a flu-like virus, but you are very far from them. It is natural they would worry more than if you were with them in Ireland and could see you for themselves.' He didn't add that if they had seen Victoria at her worst, worry would easily have turned into the same cold panic that had engulfed him all those years ago, and had come perilously close to engulfing him again.

Doubt clouded her eyes but then she gave another tired smile. 'You think?'

'Trust me. It is the same for me with my family.'

She held his gaze a moment longer then nodded as if reassured, which he found odd but didn't comment on. It would be a while before Victoria was fully herself again.

'Shall I put the television on?'

Her face contorted in a suppressed yawn. 'Only if you want to watch something.'

'You want to lie back down?'

The next yawn refused to be suppressed. She caught it with her hand and gave an apologetic smile that tugged at his heart.

Fortifying himself with the mental blocks needed to get on the bed with her, he put his arm around her and held her steady while removing the pillows he'd propped behind her.

'What's happening with the storm?' she asked sleepily as she lay back down.

Making a heroic effort not to pay any attention to the movement of her breasts as she made herself comfortable, he pulled the duvet up to her shoulders. 'Still doing storm things. They are saying we should expect another two or three days of it.'

'That long?' Her eyes looked troubled. 'I should move to a guest room and let you have your bed back.'

He gave a dismissive shake of his head. 'We can think about that tomorrow. For now, rest and build your strength. The sofa is perfectly adequate for me to sleep on.'

'Don't do that,' she pleaded. 'Take one of the guest beds.'

'If I sleep in a guest room, how will I know if you need me in the night?' He forced a preen into his voice. 'I know I am a superhero but I cannot see through walls.'

He anticipated eyes dancing with amusement at this, hoped too for a quip that would release some of the tension he'd been unable to stop building at the feel of her soft warmth pressed against him. Neither occurred.

The eyes glued to his…for the first time he couldn't prevent his brain recognising what a beautiful hazel colour they were…simply stared. The lips he'd never allowed himself to register as being wide and plump until his finger had brushed against the bottom one pulled in, her cheeks…such high cheekbones she had…sucking in with them.

Her hand slipped out of the duvet and, as it had done all those hours ago, reached for him. 'Thank you,' she whispered.

It was the soft sincerity of her gratitude that made his chest swell all over again and made him swallow before he captured the opened hand in his own. *'Prego.'*

The sensation that seeped through his skin as her fingers wrapped around his…

There was a slight tremor in her lips before she pulled a smile to her face and said, 'Don't think this means I've changed my mind about quitting.'

He brought her hand to his mouth and kissed her fingers before he even knew he was going to do it.

CHAPTER FIVE

'WE NEED TO change the bedsheets,' Marcello declared the next morning. Victoria's recovery was continuing. She'd slept soundly through the night without any spike in temperature and had woken only once for painkillers, for what she'd described as 'a pneumatic drill in my head'. In the hours she'd been awake, she'd eaten two of the croissants he'd found in the freezer, baked for the stated time and only slightly burned for breakfast, drunk two cups of tea from a box the concierge had provided from some hidden stash, brushed her teeth, and taken only half the pain relief allowed. Her colour was steadily improving, the musical lilt of her voice growing stronger too.

She threw him the dubious expression he'd seen many times when she'd been reading through start-up investment pitches. 'Have you ever changed bedsheets before?'

'I have seen it done. Do you need help getting out of bed?'

She'd made a few bathroom breaks with Marcello assisting her to and from the door, but had insisted on doing her last visit solo. In turn, he'd insisted on walking beside her so she could grab him if she felt her legs buckling.

He'd imagined not having to touch her would make the journey from bed to bathroom easier. He'd been wrong. Watching her move across the room was as difficult as having her soft body leaning into him.

'I can manage.' She pulled the duvet off her lap and slowly twisted her legs round until her feet hit the floor.

As with every other occasion that Victoria had left the bed, Marcello did his best to tune out the body clad only in a white T-shirt. It was a feat that was becoming harder with practice, not easier, and he expelled relief that her gait was stronger than the last time, her steps more assured.

She padded slowly past him, her incredible body on full display, the full breasts… God in heaven, he could not stop himself from fantasising about taking them in his mouth…gently moving beneath his T-shirt, the tips jutting out at the perfect angle… And that large, peachy bottom, and those *legs*. Victoria had the hourglass figure of the iconic Italian actress whose films his mother had dieted on in his youth, and as she settled on the sofa and drew her knees up to her belly, he could not stop himself from wondering if the pubis hidden behind the black cotton was the same shade of deep red as her hair or the darker, browner shade of her eyebrows.

His veins, already thick with the awareness alive in him from his waking moment, rose in temperature, and a deep stab of desire burned through his loins.

Turning his face away, he closed his eyes and breathed deeply, swallowing back the moisture filling his mouth.

If she could read his mind she would be furious with him. Sickened.

He was sickened with himself. Sickened that he could not stop his thoughts going to all the forbidden places. Sickened that he was attuned to her in a way he had no right to be. Sickened, too, that it was becoming increasingly hard to control his physical responses around her.

Desire for his executive assistant, the woman who'd become indispensable to him, had grabbed him by the throat and was refusing to let go.

Her phone rang. He picked it up off the bedside table and dropped it on the sofa beside the bottom that the urge to squeeze whenever she was leant against him was becoming intolerable to live with.

'I will get the bedding,' he muttered, already striding to the door.

This couldn't go on. He needed to create some physical distance between them, starting now.

Victoria stared at the door Marcello had just disappeared out of and knew she hadn't imagined the shortness in the way he'd just spoken. Knew too that she hadn't imagined the stiffening in his body when she'd walked past him.

Since she'd woken that morning, she'd felt a lot more with it and much less dopey. More attuned to Marcello's mood. Something was off with him. It was nothing she could put a finger on, more a feeling. There was a tension about him. His attentiveness hadn't dipped but his good humour was starting to feel forced.

Wasn't there a saying about guests being like fish and going off after three days? she thought miserably as she answered her grandmother's call. She didn't know if her family were more worried about her illness or the storm, but at least she could truthfully assure them—her grandmother put her on loud speaker so everyone could join in the conversation whether they wanted to or not—that she was on the mend. There was a weariness in her bones but the exhaustion that had cloaked her these last few days had finally lifted.

The storm, though, had gained a second wind and seemed intent on causing as much destruction as possible. The wind itself had dropped but the blizzard continued unabated. To leave Marcello's apartment, even by car, would be akin to pressing self-destruct.

She was in no position to leave his apartment but she could move to one of the guest rooms, she decided when the call with her family ended. Give Marcello his room back. Give him the space away from her she sensed he needed.

And it would give her needed space away from him too. Because no matter how often she told herself that it was gratitude causing her chest to swell whenever she looked at him, gratitude did not explain why her pulses soared whenever he neared her or why her breaths shortened whenever he touched her, or explain the steady burn deep in her pelvis whenever her shortened breaths inhaled his scent.

She couldn't lie to herself any more. She was attracted to Marcello. Deeply attracted.

She could cry.

Of all the people in the world to experience her first real desire for, Marcello was the worst. No woman with a single brain cell got involved with him expecting it to last longer than five minutes.

And now she could laugh. Why was she thinking such things?

As if she'd be stupid enough to give her virginity to him… Oh, God, why did she just think that?

If he could read her mind, he'd be embarrassed for her. Worse, he'd pity her.

She would never be able to look him in the eye again.

Their working relationship would be ruined.

If he knew the feelings that were bubbling inside her for him, she'd have no choice but to leave his employment for real. They certainly weren't reciprocated. She should be grateful for this. She *was* grateful. In all her imaginings, she'd never considered that the first time she got virtually naked with a man would be through sickness. Marcello's matter-of-fact attitude about it all meant the mortification she would otherwise be experiencing to remember how he'd undressed her, however vague those memories were, never had the chance to take off. She'd spent days in his company wearing nothing but an oversized white T-shirt one glance in a mirror confirmed left little to the imagination, and he'd not given a single sign that he'd noticed.

Facts were facts, and the fact was Marcello never had seen and never would see her as a woman, so more fool her for letting her lowered defences addle her brain enough to finally see him for the drop-dead sexy man he was.

The bedroom door opened.

Her heart kicked against her ribs.

He flashed a smile.

'I couldn't find fresh bedding so I have taken the bedding from the other guest room,' he said as he dumped his haul on the armchair. 'They are all clean.'

Of course they were clean, she told herself, desperately trying to think of something to take her mind from the fact her pulses were going haywire. One of Marcello's little quirks was an insistence of having his bedsheets changed daily. Victoria imagined he'd mentally preened numerous times since finding himself temporarily staff-less at stoically sleeping in the same bedding for longer than a night. She doubted it would have occurred to him to try laundering them himself, a thought that days ago would have made her eyes roll but now filled her chest with an emotion she couldn't begin to understand and made her haywire pulses thrash even louder in her ears.

He gathered all the pillows she'd slept on. 'Now that you are well enough to sleep without supervision, I will move to a guest room.' A brief skim of his eyes to hers and another flash of his teeth. 'This body of a superhero demands a bed to sleep in.'

The swelling in her chest deflated and sank to the pit of her stomach. So she hadn't imagined it. He really was craving space away from her.

Trying to fake amusement so he wouldn't sense the dejection she would hate him to see, she said as lightly as she could manage, 'Superheroes deserve their own beds. *I'll* move to the guest room.'

And be forced to sleep in the bed Victoria had lain over every inch of, and rest his head on pillows her head had rested on? Marcello was trying to drive her out of his senses, not open himself to having her delve deeper into them. He wasn't a masochist. A few nights in the guest room and then the blizzard would be over, Victoria would return to her own apartment and he would return to his bed without fresh memories of her lying in it.

'Victoria, when a man is playing the role of superhero he does not make the recovering heroine move rooms,' he said sternly. 'I need you to stay here so you can fully appreciate my selflessness.'

Thankful for a task that demanded his attention and distracted his gaze from the beautiful, semi-clad woman curled on his sofa, he yanked at the under-sheet until it submitted and pinged free. He imagined his mother's reaction at his feat of separating bedsheet from mattress. His ex-wife too, he thought, would be lost for words. He might message Livia and tell her, but…no. It would only lead to questions and he would be unable to give any answer she wanted to hear.

He'd visited her on Christmas Day. Drank a glass of wine with her and her new husband. Not so new now. Six years and two children together. Beautiful, healthy children. Marcello was happy for her. She deserved the happiness she'd found. Livia had found the courage to put her heart on the line again.

For all his genuine happiness for her though, Marcello could never do the same. There was no coming back from the pain he'd gone through. Not for him.

He still didn't know why he'd woken Christmas morning in his parents' guest bedroom with the urge to see his ex-wife. They'd kept in touch through the years but he hadn't seen her since the divorce was finalised and they'd shared one last meal in a concerted effort to part as friends. He could only assume his grandfather giving him his grandmother's engagement ring on Christmas Eve had set something off in him. He'd known his mother was behind the well-meant gesture so had gracefully accepted the ring, but it had made a difficult time of the year more so.

It was when Livia had been seeing him off from her home and they'd finally been alone that she'd taken his hand and looked him in the eye with a sympathetic smile. 'You are allowed to move on too, Marcello,' she'd said.

'I'm good,' he'd replied, not pretending not to know what she was talking about.

'Then why did you come here?'

He hadn't been able to answer that then and couldn't answer it now. All he'd known as he'd walked back to his car was that he'd needed to hear Victoria's musical lilt and so he'd called her, and for the few minutes they'd spoken, a little of the tightness he'd woken with in his chest had eased. It had been enough to sustain him through a day that always felt more bitter than sweet, a day when the gap in his life and the hole in his heart always felt that much more acute.

He reached for the clean under-sheet and said to the woman whose musical voice had raised a smile on a day his cheek muscles rarely worked without effort, 'Was that your family on the phone?'

'Yes.' It was the first time she'd spoken to any of them other than her grandma since New Year's Day, Victoria realised with a pang. Since she'd moved to Manhattan, the supposed glamour of her life meant things had improved immeasurably when she returned home for visits, her family agog to hear stories about her demanding boss and the city that never slept. But that was only when she was home. Out of sight still meant out of mind. 'I promised Grandma Brigit that you have been superhuman in your care of me.'

The only wonder was that it had taken so long for the man used to having other people cater to his every need to get fed up of playing nursemaid.

He actually caught her eye at this, a look of astonishment on his face. 'The fire-breathing dragon is called Brigit? The same as the storm?'

She grinned. 'Very apt, isn't it?'

'Is she as scary in real life as she is on the phone?'

'Much worse,' she assured him. 'When my sister Mags brought her first boyfriend home, Grandma terrified him so much that he never came back. None of my sisters ever brought a boyfriend home after that, not unless they were certain she'd gone out.'

'She lived with you?'

Watching him wrestle the clean under-sheet with the face of a man wrestling his personal nemesis elicited such a swell of emotion in her that she had to swallow it to answer. 'My granddaddy died when I was a baby. She moved in with us then.'

The way she said *granddaddy*, with the fullness of her Irish brogue, made Marcello grin improbably.

'What?' she asked, noticing.

He shook his head and continued fighting the ridiculous under-sheet. 'Nothing. So you grew up living with the fire-breathing dragon?'

'I did.'

He resisted a quip about Victoria keeping her boyfriends away. This current easy conversation was good. The last thing he wanted was to dip into the dangerous territory of thinking about her romantic life.

Even before he'd developed these disturbing feelings for her, Marcello had known he would cheerfully sabotage any kind of romantic life Victoria had until science found a way to clone her for him. He'd only felt compelled to do it once, the one date she'd mentioned to him: her theatre date. He'd taken great delight in imagining her date as an acne-riddled, pot-bellied bore, then experienced even greater delight that her date must have been as boring as he'd hoped when she left him stranded at the theatre so she could help Marcello find his missing Montblanc.

If he'd known about Grandma Brigit sooner, he'd have offered to pay for her to move in with Victoria as a guard dog to keep suitors away until the scientists had honed their human cloning technique.

'You must have spent your childhood hiding under your bed from her,' he said.

She laughed lightly. 'My sisters would disagree but she wasn't that bad. Saying that, I was always the closest to her.'

'She let you get close without burning you to a crisp?' he asked in fake astonishment.

Her smile was wry. 'I suffered my share of singes but…' She was silent a long moment. 'I think it's because I was a baby when she came to live with us. I was a distraction for her grief at losing my granddaddy. Or a comfort. I don't know. I don't remember, what with only being a baby. But she always looked out for me. Stopped me always being swallowed up by my sisters.'

Marcello felt a pang of empathy for the fire-breathing dragon. There was only one lesson in life he would sell his soul to have never experienced, and that was grief.

'What do you mean about being swallowed up?'

She was silent another long moment before quietly saying, 'I'm the second youngest of five girls. I had no clearly defined role in the pack. I wasn't the oldest or the baby—Sinead came eleven months after me—or even the rebellious middle child. I was the one whose name no one could get right first time. If Mum wanted me, she'd always call one of my sisters' names first, which I know is normal but it always felt like I was the only one whose name wasn't on the tip of her tongue, the insignificant one. I could hide in my room for hours and she wouldn't even notice I wasn't there.

'Grandma was terrifying but she knew exactly who I was. She never forgot me or my name.'

An image danced in his mind of a pretty little redhead sitting on a floor, stepped over and unnoticed by the crowd surrounding her.

Blinking the image away, his stare was caught by the grown, beautiful redhead curled on his bedroom sofa, the beautiful redhead whose stifled laughter had stayed at the forefront of his memories like a warm glow for months before he'd grabbed the opportunity to employ her.

'There is nothing forgettable about you, Victoria,' he said with simple honesty.

Her eyes widened.

There was an almost imperceptible rise of her shoulders and then, just as he was about to jerk his stare away, he saw it.

The dark pulsing in her eyes and the creep of colour over her cheeks.

A bolt of electricity exploded in his chest.

Silence chimed loudly.

The hazel eyes widened into orbs. A trembling hand pressed against her breast…

Suddenly fighting for breath, Marcello wrenched his stare to the sheet gripped tightly in his hand. Auto-pilot kicked in and, the room in pitch silence, he fought the under-sheet until it submitted, then worked quickly to place the pillows and duvet from the guest room onto the bed, all the while trying to convince himself that he hadn't just seen what he'd seen. Told himself it had been a trick of the light. A manifestation of his desire in the form of an illusion.

He had to force himself to look at her again. Had to clear his throat to speak. 'I need to make some calls. I won't be far, just in the office.' The office he'd had a second desk added to so Victoria could work from the apartment when needed. 'Do you need anything?'

Even darker colour stained her cheeks and she hastily turned her face away and shook her head.

'Bene.'

He left the room without another word.

Victoria's knees were drawn to her chin, her mouth pressed tight against them.

Her heart was racing.

He'd seen.

Marcello had seen.

Oh, God.

Hot blood was whooshing in her head.

She couldn't think what to do.

He'd *seen*. She knew it.

It had been the starkness in both his expression and voice when he'd said there was nothing forgettable about her. The emotion that had ballooned in her…

In that moment she'd been helpless to stop her burgeoning feelings from showing on her face, and he'd *seen* it. And he'd recognised it for what it was. She knew it. There was no hiding it now. From either of them.

Oh, God, the pained look that had flashed over him.

He'd been unable to get away from her fast enough.

What was she going to do?

More sleep, she decided desperately. Bury herself in oblivion until it was safe to leave the apartment.

The weakness in her legs on her walk to the bed had nothing to do with the virus she'd been fighting.

Whether it was all the sleep she'd had since falling ill or the electrical current zinging in her veins, the oblivion she hankered for refused to come. Even burying her head under the pillow didn't help. All she could see was Marcello's pained expression.

'Victoria?'

She threw the pillow off and whipped her face towards the door.

Marcello was standing on the threshold holding a tray with a bowl and a tall glass of water.

Her heart flew up her throat.

He didn't meet her stare. His shoulders rose, strong, deep olive throat moving. 'Lunch. None of the delis or restaurants are delivering still, so I am afraid you have to put up with my latest attempt at cooking.'

So that was how he was going to play it? By pretending nothing had happened?

A way out of the nightmare opened itself, and she scrambled to sit up, murmuring her thanks. If he could pretend then so could she.

He stepped into the room. 'Where do you want me to put it?'

He hadn't asked that before. He always brought it to her in bed.

'The table. By the armchair. Please.' Pulling the duvet off her lap, she climbed off the bed.

Lips tight, jaw clenched, he turned his face away from her.

For the first time since she'd fallen ill, embarrassment at her lack of clothing seared her, and as mortification engulfed her in a burning flame, she caught a glimpse of her reflection in the full-length mirror and understood why he'd turned his stare away. The light in the room had made the white T-shirt she was wearing semi-translucent.

Wishing something would fall from the sky and snatch her up and take her far away, Victoria hugged her arms across her breasts and padded to the armchair. Marcello visibly stiffened when she passed him, magnifying her awkwardness. When she went to sit, her thigh bashed into the table. In horrified slow motion, she watched the tall glass topple and hit the side of the tray with a loud crack.

The glass shattered.

In the blink of an eye, water flooded the tray, spilling onto the highly polished, expensive side table and dripping onto the Persian rug.

Could the situation be any more excruciating? she wondered despairingly as she crouched down and attempted to gather the broken shards together, mumbling an apology.

'Did any of the glass get you?' he asked tersely.

'No. It's all on the tray.'

'Then leave it. I'll get a cloth.'

His tone accelerated her despair. Marcello was the least precious man when it came to spillages and breakages.

He really was fed up of taking care of her. Probably fed up with her altogether.

'I told you to leave it,' Marcello snapped when he returned moments later with a hand towel from the bathroom and found Victoria putting all the smaller glass fragments into the larger pieces.

'It's my mess, I should clean it.'

'You have done enough.'

Her flinch made his guts clench.

Marcello knew he was being unreasonable but his clenched guts were burning. *He* was burning.

It had been hard enough dealing with and fighting his own erupting attraction when he'd believed it to be one-sided. To see it mirrored in Victoria's eyes…

Dio, he wished he could wipe what he'd seen from his mind.

If that look had come from anyone but Victoria then he'd be welcoming it. *Delighting* in it.

But Victoria wasn't just anyone. She was far from being just *anyone*. She was his Woman Friday. A purely platonic Woman Friday. He'd made damned sure of that.

He could not lose her from his life. To act on their feelings could only lead to disaster.

He had an awful sinking feeling that disaster had already struck.

He'd had to brace himself just to walk back into the bedroom with her lunch, had had to set a clear path in his mind for dealing with it: he would deliver food to wherever she wanted and then, once she was settled and comfortable, he would leave.

If not for the smashed glass he'd already be back at his computer immersing himself in work.

Or trying to.

What was it they said about the best-laid plans? he thought grimly, crouching beside her and doing everything humanly possible to tune out the closeness of the body driving him to distraction.

'I never asked to get ill,' she snapped back, pinching another small shard and dropping it with the others.

He gritted his teeth. 'I never said you did.'

'You just implied it.'

Dio, he should be celebrating that she was enough of herself to argue with him; the memory of that long night when he'd had grips of fear that she'd never argue with him again still fresh, but the sleeve of her T-shirt brushed against his arm as she reached over to pinch another shard and he knew that if he looked down, he'd find the hem had risen higher up her thigh and would be skimming the bottom his fingers wouldn't quit yearning to touch.

'Will you get out of my way and let me clear this up?' he demanded roughly, lifting the tray and running the towel over the table to soak up the spilt water.

'Will you stop talking to me like you think I'm an annoyance?'

'Then stop being annoying.' Feeling her angry… hurt…stare on him, Marcello gritted his teeth even harder. He would swear he heard her grit her teeth too.

'I'm not going to throw myself at you, you know,' she said tautly.

His guts kicked in rhythm with his heart. Breathing heavily, he tightened his grip on the towel. 'Do not go there, Victoria.'

Some things should never be spoken of. Never openly acknowledged.

He felt her shift. Knew without looking that she'd untucked her calves from beneath her and was now sitting on her damnably beautiful bottom.

'Why not when that's what this is all about?' she retorted. ‘Because it is, isn’t it?’ There was a catch in her musical lilt. ‘I know you saw it, but I know perfectly well that you don’t see me in the same way, so unless you’re deliberately trying to hurt me, you don’t have to make your revulsion so blindingly obvious.’

CHAPTER SIX

THE CLEAR BLUE eyes Victoria had always been able to read so well suddenly snapped onto hers. They glittered with a darkness that turned her stomach to mush and made the beats of her racing heart thrash.

She forced herself to gaze into the darkness. She didn't have to force the words that came next. 'Do you think I *wanted* to become attracted to you?' Something was building in her chest, a sob or laughter, she didn't know, but she pinched the bridge of her nose in a valiant attempt to stop it escaping. 'Never mind that you're my boss—were my boss—you'd give Casanova a run for his money.' A short bark of laughter escaped at the same moment a tear spilled over. 'Whatever stupid feelings have developed on my part are just a side-effect of the virus, and even if the attraction was returned I would never be stupid enough to act on it, so—'

'For God's sake, Victoria, are you *blind*?' Slamming a hand on the floor beside her thigh, he leaned his taut face down to hers. 'How can you not see it?'

Trembling, trapped in Marcello's stare, she had no choice but to stare even deeper into the darkness that she suddenly saw with a kick in her heart wasn't darkness at all, but a swirling vortex pulsing a mirror of what she was feeling.

The world moved around her. Sensation throbbed in her chest, like he'd squeezed her heart with his bare hand.

As if she were a magnet irresistibly drawn to his hypnotic pull, her face moved closer to his. She could hardly raise her voice above a whisper. 'Then why…?'

The pained look she'd seen earlier flashed over his rugged features. The look she'd interpreted as a mixture of disgust and pity… 'Why do you think?'

But the world was moving too fast around her to think with any coherence. The realisation that her feelings were shared was hitting her in an ever increasing crescendo of waves. Now that she could see it, it was all she could see, right there in the depths of the blue eyes glittering with his desire for her.

He tilted his head. Now he was the one to bring his face closer.

His voice dropped. 'I do not want to hurt you, Victoria, and I do not want to lose you. I want you by my side for the rest of my professional life. To act on our feelings…' He inhaled deeply through his nose. His exhale landed like a whisper against her mouth. 'I have done marriage. You know that, don't you?'

It was a statement rather than a question.

Her chest hitching, she nodded.

The intensity of his stare deepened. 'I will never

marry again. I will never live with anyone again. I have committed to being a bachelor for the rest of my life and I date from a pool of shallow vipers precisely for that reason. I can end it with one message and move on without a second of guilt or regret. You deserve so much more than to be treated like that, and your friendship and value as my right-hand woman are worth more to me than any short-lived fling.'

It wasn't just the hoarse delivery of his words compelling her to listen but the demons glimmering in his pulsing eyes. The demons she'd always sensed lived beneath his affable exterior. Marcello's demons, showing themselves to warn her away.

'You've given it a lot of thought,' she said, shaken at the depth of emotion she was seeing.

'I have thought of nothing else since my eyes opened to just how beautiful you are.'

Victoria's shoulders slumped. Her eyes closed. She tried to breathe through the smashing of her heart and the ripples of its beats.

The only people who'd called her beautiful before were drunken, lecherous men. To hear it from Marcello filled her with such an *ache*…

Oh, this was *madness*! It felt like only five minutes ago that all the reasons he'd just laid out to her had already been firmly lodged in her mind. She hadn't needed telling. She'd known only fools let themselves fall for Marcello Guardiola.

And now she was that fool. She'd woken from the

worst illness of her life and gazed at him sprawled out on the sofa he'd been keeping watch over her from, and felt something fundamental shift inside her.

But he was right. However deep the longing to press her hand against his stubbly cheek and breathe in the scent of his skin and the undertones of his cologne deep into her lungs, and however deep the burning yearning to fuse herself to him, to act on her feelings would be to press self-destruct on her whole life.

Pride filling her with resolve, she lifted her gaze back to him. 'I think you're forgetting something.'

His shoulders rose. 'What is that?'

'I don't work for you any more.'

For the first time since the glass shattered, the tautness of his features relaxed and, though his eyes didn't lose an ounce of their intensity, the lines around them crinkled. 'Yes, you do. And I will pay any price to keep you.'

And if that meant keeping his desire contained then that was how it had to be. Marcello would not hurt Victoria for anything. He would not lose her for anything.

Victoria sat on the sill staring out of a bedroom window. The wind had picked up again. If she strained her ears she could imagine its howl. The sun had set. Another night under the same roof as Marcello was closing in.

A light tap on the door made her heart thump. She tightened the sash of his robe, taken earlier from the back of the bathroom door, and took a deep breath to compose herself before turning to face him.

He stood at the threshold, arms loosely crossed around his chest. It was the same stance he'd adopted when he'd checked in on her a few hours earlier. As with earlier, he made no comment about her wearing his robe. But he'd noticed. She knew he had. It had been in the flare of his eyes before he'd turned his stare away.

This time he kept his gaze on her. 'I am going to work on my cooking skills. Is there anything you want for dinner?'

'Anything that's readymade works for me,' she managed to jest. Lunch had gone in the bin. Once the broken glass had been cleared, she'd tried the pasta he'd made for her. It had been inedible and not just because it was cold. Her stomach had been too tense and knotted to accept his offer of something else. He hadn't forced the issue. He'd retreated to his office and given them the space they both needed.

He might as well have brought his computer into the bedroom.

He'd kept the bedroom door open so she could call if she needed him. His voice had carried into the room from his office. The words of his conversations had been indistinguishable but the effect of them a torment. She'd never known a distant voice could soak through skin and squeeze a heart.

His laughter was as forced as the bonhomie they were both faking. 'No more pasta?'

She made herself smile. 'Only if you want to kill me off.'

More forced laughter. 'You will be pleased to know the storm is expected to ease soon. I am making arrangements for a snowplough to be sent to collect Bernard in the morning.'

'The chef?'

He nodded. 'And some cleaners.'

'*You're* making the arrangements?'

He preened. 'I know. There is no end to my talents.'

She only had to half force a snigger at this. 'How are Christina and Patrick doing?'

'They are improved but they are not recovering as quickly as you…' A line creased his forehead. 'You *are* still feeling improvement?'

'I'm getting stronger by the hour.'

His head inclined. *'Bene.'* He straightened and made to leave.

'I'm going to take a quick bath if that's okay?' she said quickly, before she lost her nerve. For someone who showered twice daily, Victoria was acutely aware she hadn't bathed since falling ill. While her strength was increasing by the hour, her yearning to feel clean was accelerating by the minute.

There was a slight stiffening of Marcello's shoulders. The air, already laden with tension, thickened. 'You are sure you feel strong enough?'

She nodded.

He lifted his stiff shoulders into a shrug. 'Help yourself to whatever you need. Clean T-shirts are in drawers to the left of the dressing room door. I would offer you jeans to wear too but…'

He didn't need to finish his sentence. They both knew they were both thinking it. There was no way Victoria was going to get a pair of jeans designed for his snake hips past her curves.

His breathing had become heavy. His throat moved before another taut smile curved his cheeks. 'Food in an hour?'

'If I must.'

The smile widened into something more genuine. He tapped the side of his forehead with two of his fingers. 'Do not drown.'

'I'll try not to.'

Victoria had never been in Marcello's dressing room before. She'd seen glimpses of it but those glimpses had failed to convey its vastness. Stepping into it reminded her of walking into that tailor's shop on Bond Street with him. The difference was in size. Marcello's dressing room had twice the floor space. It smelled crisper too. Unthinkingly, she rubbed her nose into the collar of his robe and breathed in the underlying scent of his cologne. She'd put it on only to cover her flesh and make it easier for the two of them to be with each other. After spending days in his T-shirt, she hadn't expected to feel such intimacy wearing his robe. Hadn't expected it to feel like an embrace.

Expelling the breath, she closed her eyes.

If Marcello was right and the storm did ease overnight, then that meant it should soon be safe for her to leave. If she continued improving as she was then, come the morning, she would dig her clothes out of the laundry pile Marcello had added them to. Get a lift on the snowplough. Return to her apartment. Hope the physical distance from him gave her the head space needed to decide what she should do next.

Resign officially or stay and hope for the best?

She couldn't think clearly in Marcello's home, wearing his clothes and feeling his presence like a vibration in her skin.

Selecting a grey T-shirt, she left the dressing room for his en suite. Another room stamped as essentially Marcello. As masculine a bathroom as could be imagined. Charcoal tiled walls. Hard black flooring. A huge walk-in shower that could be mistaken for a cave. Even the chaise longue that separated the shower side from the rolltop bath was black leather, and as she poured the citrus-scented bubble bath into the gushing water, it came to her again that he hadn't marked every single part of his apartment with his own stamp for aesthetic reasons, but as a warning to the many women he'd invited into it.

Do not get close.

Marcello tried to focus on the food he'd selected and laid out before him on the kitchen island. Tried not to think that at this exact moment, Victoria was naked in the bath.

In the back of his mind had been the unacknowledged knowledge that at some point Victoria would feel well enough to want to shower. A shower would have been hard enough to handle. A bath was a whole different level of torture.

He'd stayed in his office while she ran it. Had somehow heard over the blood roaring in his ears the sloshing of water as she'd stepped into it. Only when he'd assured himself that she was safely settled did he move downstairs to the kitchen, the furthest point in his apartment from his en suite. With the electricity racing through his veins it could be the other side of the bathroom wall.

He ripped the seal around the steaks with his bare hands and placed them on the heated pan as the Internet instructed. Washing his hands, he closed his eyes in another effort to eradicate the image of Victoria submerged in the bath. Naked. Fully naked. Water swirling around her breasts and pubis…

He groaned and dragged his wet fingers through his hair.

Earlier, it had taken superhuman control to back away from her but there was no self-control of his mind. Not any more.

The so very erotic images behind his eyelids became suddenly distorted.

Snapping his eyes back open, he found himself in darkness.

Victoria had been trying to summon the strength to get out of the bath when the lights extinguished.

It wasn't physical strength she'd been seeking but the mental strength needed to leave this temporary sanctuary from Marcello and deal with seeing him again. Talking to him. Pretending.

Pretending that when the storm passed and she'd fully recovered, things could go back to how they used to be.

And then she found herself lying in the bath in the pitch black.

The door was closed. No light spilled through the cracks from the bedroom. It must be a full-blown power cut. She'd closed, too, the expertly fitted blinds. No residual light from the outside could penetrate it.

Groping carefully for the rolled sides, she sat up and called Marcello's name. The bathwater had been cooling and now goosebumps flecked her skin.

She hugged her knees and called his name again. She'd put a towel on the chaise longue but couldn't even make out its shadow.

And then she heard her name.

'I'm still in the bath,' she called back.

'Are you okay?' His voice came from behind the door.

'Yes, but I can't see anything at all.'

The door opened. A circle of orange light filled the doorway. It took a moment for her brain to catch up and see it was the torch from Marcello's phone. Of him, she could see nothing, not even his outline.

'There has been a power cut,' his disembodied voice informed her grimly. 'From what I can see, most of Central Park is down.'

Acutely aware that he could see her, she covered her breasts and tried to speak normally. 'Doesn't the building have a back-up generator?'

'I would assume so. I will check with the concierge once you're out of the bath. Can you see enough to get out safely?'

The orange glow now coming from the doorway was emanating just enough light by the bath to create shadows. 'I think so.'

He must have picked up on her uncertainty. The light moved closer until its source stopped by the double sink. 'Better?'

'Yes…' She swallowed and strove even harder for normality in her voice, as if what she was about to ask were an everyday occurrence. 'Can you pass me the towel please? It's on the chaise longue.'

'Sure.'

The light source moved again. She saw the gleam of an outstretched arm at the same moment she heard the rustle of a bath towel being lifted.

The light moved closer.

She reached for the towel. Once she had it in her clasp, the light source retreated a few steps.

'I will stay close in case you need me,' he said tightly.

She nodded and tried to open her throat to breathe. The light from the phone had put her under a dimly glowing spotlight. The man behind it was still indistinguishable but she could feel him through the vibrations of her naked skin that no longer felt cold. Could hear the long pauses between each of his breaths…

Marcello turned his face from her. He could not turn off the rest of his senses.

Water sloshed and, as much as he tried to think about anything else, all he could see in his mind's eye was the illuminated figure in the bath tub rising slowly to her feet.

He'd had to brace himself before entering the bathroom knowing it would be impossible to avoid Victoria's nakedness. And so it had proved. Her wet hair, part covering her breasts, had contrasted strongly with the luminescence of her skin. A mermaid come to life. A siren leading a man to danger…

'Can I borrow your hand while I step out, please?' she whispered.

Everything inside him contracted sharply then pulsed in a rush. He had to tighten his grip on the phone before he could force the steps needed to reach her side.

Closing his eyes, he reached out to her and did his damnedest to banish the image of Victoria in full, curvaceous naked bloom. It was futile. One glance had etched in his retinas. Even with only the dim torchlight, that one glance had been enough to see that the soft down of hair between her legs was the same beautiful shade of red as the hair on her head.

Dio, his blood had never pumped so hard.

The tips of their fingers connected. Electricity crackled through his skin and deep into his loins.

The silence as their hands clasped together was so complete he could hear the individual droplets of water run off Victoria's naked skin and splash back into the bath.

The loudest sound, though, came from the drum of his heart beating in his ears.

The heat of the water had opened her pores. His lungs opened to breathe in the scent clinging to her. A scent that should be masculine but on Victoria's skin became something distinctly feminine. Distinctly Victoria.

Awareness and desire had never thrummed so deeply, and he clenched his jaw tighter than he'd ever clenched it before in an effort to control it. Never in his whole life had he fought such a war with his own body.

Never in the entirety of her life had Victoria been so conscious of the skin that wrapped her body, aware that it was a living, breathing organ in its own right. It was breathing in Marcello, her hidden Adonis. Only the hand holding her so securely had emerged from the shadows but she could feel the substance vibrating from his own cloak of flesh.

Pulses thrashing wildly, she lifted her leg over the bath.

The floor was lower than anticipated and the extra depth as her foot searched for hard floor caught her unawares and she wobbled, would have fallen into an ungainly heap if Marcello hadn't wound an arm around her waist to steady her. A moment later he'd lifted her out of the bath.

The phone slipped from his hand at the same moment both her feet made contact with the floor. She had only a dim awareness of the clunk it made because in an instant her thrashing pulses ran out of control and she lost the ability to think coherently.

The towel she'd wrapped around herself had slipped to her waist and she was pressed against Marcello, pressed so tightly her breasts were squashed against his hard chest. His hands were flat against the small of her naked back, the pads of his fingers biting into her flesh.

And she was clinging to him. One hand was holding his shoulder, the other gripping the side of his waist. The pads of her fingers were biting as hard into him as his fingers bit into her.

Blood zoomed through her in a rush, its heat fizzing and throbbing through her skin, deep into her bones and into the places kept secret even from herself. Helpless to do anything else, she lifted her face.

The light from the phone on the floor arched upwards and suffused them both in the spotlight of its glow. Marcello's chiselled jaw was as rigid as his body holding her so securely and yet so stiffly. His eyes, though, locked straight onto hers. If she'd had any air left, the emotion and hunger contained in them would have knocked it out of her.

An age passed before his nostrils flared and he expelled a short but heavy breath. It danced over her forehead like a caress.

'Walk away, Victoria,' he muttered raggedly, his stare continuing to burn into her.

She rose onto her toes without thought.

His eyes became hooded, his breathing even heavier. One hand dragged slowly up her back. 'Walk away. Walk away now.'

Shivers racing down her spine at the pleasure of his touch, unable to tear her stare from his, she slowly slipped her fingers beneath his T-shirt. His warm skin was smooth. Heavenly.

His eyes closed as if in prayer. His other hand moved, fingers sliding beneath the fallen towel to clasp her bottom. His stare fixing back on hers, he made a barely perceptible twist of his hips and clasped her tighter.

She gave a short gasp as the towel fell to the floor and his hardness pressed into her naked abdomen.

'Walk away, Victoria,' he urged hoarsely even as he pressed his thigh between her legs to drive his hardness tighter against her and his taut, pained face inched closer. 'Walk away…' his mouth was so close his hot breath soaked into her lips '…before it's too late.'

Desire pulsed through the very fabric of her being and, her hand now palming the back of Marcello's neck and her fingers tugging at the dark hair at the base of his skull, it was all she could do to stay on her feet. All those long months of pretending to herself…lying…that Marcello meant nothing more to her than the man who paid her salary had been blown away. She'd wanted him from that very first meeting, when he'd walked into her then boss's office with an arrogant swagger she would have hated him for if he hadn't captured her gaze with those blue eyes flashing a twinkle that had made her insides melt.

His procession of lovers…she'd hated them all because deep down she'd been jealous of them. All of them. It had made her *burn* to imagine them in his bed, and, whatever happened now, she would always feel that irrational burn of jealousy. But now she would know it for what it was. Pandora's box had been opened and she could no more keep its contents contained than she could stop the tides from turning.

Whatever happened now, she was going to be hurt. That was her fate. You didn't fall for Marcello Guardiola and expect a happy ending. The most she could hope for was a happy-for-now.

She'd imagined he would be the worst person in the world to fall ill with when he'd turned out to be the best. If just to be held by him like this felt like heaven then…

She sighed against his mouth before staring deep into his eyes and whispering, 'It's already too late.'

CHAPTER SEVEN

It was the sweetness of Victoria's hot breath falling against his lips and onto his tongue that swamped the last of Marcello's resistance. With a groan of surrender, he pressed his mouth to hers.

If he hadn't already succumbed, the first sweep of her tongue against his would have incinerated his resolve. Wrapping his arms tightly around her, he devoured her pliant softness with hungry kisses that sent thrills licking through his entire being. *Dio*, her lips…soft succulence contrasting headily with the hard, passionate ardour of her responses. He was plundering heaven, and heaven was welcoming the plunder with soft moans and nails scraping into his skull. *Dio*, even her skin when he rubbed his cheek against hers felt like erotic satin.

Biting with barely disguised restraint at her delicate ear lobe, he pulled his head back and gazed at the dimly lit face he'd been blind to the beauty of for so long he wondered how he'd been able to see at all. Exquisitely beautiful, from the mesmerising hazel eyes to the oversized lips and the pretty chin with the faintest cleft in it.

Every inch exquisite. Every inch of Victoria exquisite. The need to taste it all…

The second fusion of Marcello's lips to hers was even headier than the first. Sinking into the hard, passionate demands of his mouth and tongue, consumed by his dark taste and the sensations flickering like lightning through her skin, Victoria no longer had thoughts. All she had was Marcello; his taste, his scent, his touch, all seeping through her senses to set her alight. Even his voice when he whispered into her ear, 'Come,' soaked into her skin with the same strength as the feel of his hands sweeping down her back.

Feeling as light as the bubbles in a glass of champagne and as drunk as if she'd consumed a whole bottle of it, she let him take her hand and lead her into the darkened bedroom.

A chink of silvery light from the falling snow seeped through a gap in the heavy curtains, creating a shadowed path to the bed. Hands clasped, they walked it together. By the time they reached the head of the bed, Victoria's heart was thumping so hard that sucking in air to breathe had become impossible. Excitement churned like a sickness in her stomach.

Large hands clasped her cheeks. Marcello's face emerged from the shadows. He pressed his forehead to hers. Eyes intense, his Italian accent more pronounced than she'd ever heard it, his voice was hoarse as he whispered, 'You can still walk away, Victoria.'

Unable to speak, all she could do was shake her head.

His eyes closed. His nostrils flared. And then he moved his hands from her cheeks, straightened, and, in one fluid movement, stripped off his T-shirt and threw it to the floor.

Her heart came close to punching out of her chest. It didn't matter that it was too dark to see clearly. Every inch of his torso had been committed directly into her memory bank that lifetime ago in his office, from the flat brown nipples to the dark hair that swirled around them and snaked over the washboard abdomen and down to the place she always refused to imagine even when a throb pulsed strongly between her legs. That pulse was throbbing stronger than it ever had now, and when he removed the rest of his clothing and stood naked before her and her stare took in the shadowed length of his arousal, the pulse that followed weakened her legs. Weakened all of her…and yet somehow strengthened her.

A hand clasped the back of her head. His smouldering face hovered over hers. 'Last chance,' he whispered savagely.

Something, an instinct that came right from the feminine heart of her, had her cupping his cheeks tightly. Bringing her mouth to his, she whispered with equal savageness, 'No more chances.'

The tiniest beat passed in which time hung by a thread, and then his mouth plundered hers with a kiss so hot and demanding that her weakened legs finally buckled. Wrapping her arms around his neck, revelling in the sensation of his strong arms snaking around her back to hold her tightly to him and the feel of his arousal pressing hard into her abdomen, she moaned into his mouth.

So enraptured was she to be under this sensuous assault that she barely felt her feet leave the ground when he lifted her onto the bed. A fleeting memory came of when he'd first carried her and the embarrassment that she was too heavy to be carried like a child that had broken through the fog of the virus. But there had been safety in his arms too, she remembered with wonder. Even while the virus had been running riot in its quest to infect and incapacitate her, she'd had safety in Marcello's arms, had instinctively known he would never let her fall…

Her head fell onto the pillow. Marcello's weight covered her body, his demanding mouth swooped back on hers, and the memory dissolved as she dissolved into him.

When Marcello covered Victoria's breast with his mouth and felt the scrape of her nails down his back, the thrills of arousal coursing through his loins was strong enough to take him back two decades, to his first time, when the thrill of promised pleasure had almost tipped him over the edge before he'd even started.

That eager adolescent no longer existed. Experience had taught him control. Taught him how to give pleasure for the woman's benefit and not his own. However badly his short-lived affairs ended, he'd never had the worry that they'd left his bed unsatisfied.

The strength of his desire now was beyond anything, even that first time. The urge to make Victoria his, to thrust deep inside her and lose himself in her curvaceous softness was as strong as the hunger to devour every delicious centimetre of her flesh and uncover her every last erotic secret.

Dio, it was like he'd never caressed breasts before. The weight and fullness of Victoria's simply begged to be squeezed, the texture and taste begged to be licked and kissed and nipped…her moans of pleasure… When she cradled his head in a silent plea for more and writhed beneath him, he encircled a large nipple with a groan and gently bit, fighting the very real need to consume her whole. For the first time in his life, Marcello's need to devour had nothing to do with the giving of pleasure to satisfy his ego, but to satisfy his greed, and it was his greed for more, more of Victoria, that had him snake down to the pubis that had haunted his imagination for much longer than the days he'd pretended to himself.

He'd spent eighteen months ruthlessly refusing to think of Victoria as a woman precisely because his subconscious had known what would be unleashed. And now that denial had been unleashed, he was like a child let loose in a chocolate factory without supervision.

He would not deny himself any more. He would not deny her. For this one night he would drown in her.

Spreading her thighs, he pushed them back. Too dark to see with any clarity, he rested his face between her legs and inhaled deeply. He didn't need to see clearly, not when the memory of her naked in the bathroom was still so vivid. He could satisfy his other senses, and, with another greedy inhalation of her erotic musky scent, he laid himself down and feasted.

Victoria had lost her mind. This was beyond good. Beyond pleasure. The sporadic groans from between her legs only added to the heady wonder. Marcello was getting as much from this as she was, and, God, she'd never known it would feel like this. Be like this. Something was building inside her, a thickening beyond any climax she'd brought herself to during the lonely nights she'd tried desperately hard not to picture Marcello touching her…

She moaned loudly as he slid a finger into her heat, and then his tongue found a rhythm that had her writhing and wantonly begging him not to stop until her climax ripped through her and she could speak no more.

The ripples hadn't even begun to subside when he wrenched his face away from the source of her pleasure and crawled back up her body to cover her mouth with a deeply passionate, musky-tasting kiss. Before she could wrap her arms back around him, he was kneeling between her legs and reaching into his bedside table. A short rustling and then he was ripping into a small square foil with his teeth. He'd sheathed himself in moments and then he was pushing her thighs back again, the head of his huge arousal at the entrance of her heat.

Through the dark, she felt his stare on her as he leaned forwards and raggedly muttered, '*Dio*, Victoria, I have never wanted anyone like this.' Without a second of hesitation, he drove deep inside her with a loud, drawn-out groan.

The sharp pain made her gasp. Her right leg reflexively kicked and she came within a breath of telling him to stop.

But he'd already stilled. Breathing heavily, he whispered, 'Are you okay?'

Slowly expelling her own breath, she realised she *was* okay. More than okay. The pain had already faded and as her body stretched to accommodate him and adjusted to the delicious newness of Marcello fully inside her, the magnitude of what was happening hit her.

Marcello was inside her.

Marcello was making love to her.

Cupping the back of his head, she lifted her face for his kiss. The heat of his mouth sent sensation dancing through her and, relaxing, she slid her hand to his shoulder, closed her eyes and trusted him to take her to paradise.

When he started to move, paradise itself moved closer.

This was beyond anything Marcello had ever felt before, ever experienced. Every nerve ending was alive with sensation, every vein threaded with electricity, every sense attuned to Victoria's every touch and every breathless moan. The need to drive deeper and deeper into her tight, slick heat, to fuse himself in his entirety to her…

Her moans deepened.

'*Dio mio*, Victoria, you're incredible,' he groaned before gritting his teeth in an effort to keep control of himself, and increased the tempo of his thrusts; the need to feel and experience her climax with her as strong as the increasing desperation for his own release.

Just as he felt he couldn't hold on any more, the legs wrapped around his waist and the arms around his neck tightened and she spasmed into him and around him, crying out his name as she pulled him over the edge and into an abyss of the most intense pleasure of his life.

Victoria held Marcello tightly and tried to snatch air into her lungs. She could feel the beats of his heart thumping strongly. Hear his own struggles to find air.

He was still inside her. She wanted to keep him there and never let him go…

An impossible dream but with the bliss of her climax still tingling through her veins and skin, and his mouth hot in her hair, a dream it was impossible to deny herself from longing for.

The virus that had debilitated her had weakened her defences and given the space for feelings hidden even from herself to bloom.

They were feelings as impossible as her dream. Feelings that must never be spoken of. This blissful closeness they were sharing was a temporary, fleeting thing. In a minute or an hour or a day or a week or a month, Marcello would call time as he always did.

She'd made love to him knowing he would break her heart. He would have broken her heart even if she'd walked away as he'd urged her to do.

The darkness of the bedroom meant she didn't have to hide her dejection when he finally lifted his head and pulled himself out of her.

'I need to get rid of the condom.'

She sighed and ran her fingers lightly through his hair.

He kissed her gently and then climbed off the bed.

She missed his warmth before his feet even hit the floor.

Snuggling deep under the duvet, she tried to stop herself thinking about the day in her future when an entitled female voice called and demanded to be put straight through to him. Or, worse, the day he casually instructed her to keep an evening in his schedule free. That he'd been celibate since Jenna was little short of a miracle and a feat unlikely to be repeated. She had to be realistic about these things.

An orange light appeared from the bathroom. Phone guiding him, he strode to the bedroom door without looking at her and distantly said, 'I'm going to find matches to light a candle.'

Irrationally stung, she snuggled deeper, hugged herself tightly and willed the tears not to fall.

Looked like she wouldn't even have an hour to savour what they'd just shared.

He must be regretting it already, and it pained her to

remember how many times he'd urged her to walk away before they took things too far.

She had no idea how long she lay there, torturing herself over a future she had no control of, when he padded back into the bedroom, still using his phone as a torch. In silence, he headed to the sideboard in the corner. The angle he placed his phone while unwrapping the candle illuminated him, and she took a crumb of comfort that he hadn't bothered to cover his nakedness. Surely if he was planning to start a big 'We really shouldn't have done that and it must never happen again' conversation, he would put some clothes on?

But then, who knew how Marcello extracted himself from a woman's bed when he had no intention of sharing it with her again? Not Victoria. She'd never asked. Never wanted to know.

There was a click, and then a whoosh of blue and orange flame from what looked like a miniature flamethrower shot out from his hand and the wick of a candle caught light. Another click as he turned the miniature flamethrower off and then he turned, now illuminated by the flickering candle light, and walked towards her.

Holding the duvet tightly to her chest, she sat up.

It wasn't until he'd slid beside her, rested his back against the headboard and taken hold of her hand that she was able to take a proper breath.

It was a breath that stuck in her throat when he said in a voice too casual to be casual, 'Victoria… Tell me that wasn't your first time.'

* * *

The freezing of Victoria's hand in his answered Marcello's question.

Biting back a curse, he tipped his head back and forced himself to breathe.

When he'd come back to earth after their lovemaking, it had been the moment he'd first entered her that had rung loudest. Her gasp. The flash of uncertainty that had temporarily gripped him before he'd completely lost his mind in what they were sharing.

Even as he'd been turning the kitchen upside down searching for something to light the candle with, the thought had refused to be shaken off.

And now his worst fears had been confirmed.

Victoria had been a virgin.

This beautiful, witty, confident, highly intelligent twenty-five-year-old woman had been a virgin.

'Why didn't you tell me?' he dragged out. Something dark and acrid was bubbling in his guts.

He heard her swallow. 'Because you would have used it as an excuse to stop.'

'What the hell?' Snapping his gaze to her, he stared intently at the face only a little more discernible under the candle's illumination, but discernible enough for him to catch the defiance on it. 'Did you plan this?'

'Why would I do that?' she asked tremulously. '*How* could I do that?'

Cursing under his breath, he let get of her hand and

gripped the back of his neck. 'Why would you give your virginity to a man like me, Victoria?'

Her voice lifted. 'Because you're a professional?'

'This is not the time for jokes.'

'I know but this conversation is excruciating.' She laughed but it sounded more like a sob. 'You kept telling me to walk away, but I couldn't. It was already too late for me. And it was too late for you too—if it wasn't, *you'd* have walked away. If I'd told you I was a virgin then…' She gave another sobbed laugh. 'What I'm currently feeling for you is something I've wanted to feel my entire life.'

The dark acridity in his guts intensified, the impending sense of disaster back with a vengeance. 'I cannot give you anything more than this.'

'I *know*,' she stated vehemently, sitting even straighter. 'I know that better than anyone, but I also know that our working relationship as we've always known it was over the moment this thing between us became impossible to ignore, and to think we could just carry on as if it weren't this enormous white elephant between us is for the fairies. But just because I was a virgin doesn't change anything. You've been straight with me about your feelings on relationships and stuff and I haven't wilfully ignored them. The only reason you're acting the way you are now is because you're afraid my virginity means I'm going to suddenly expect a ring on my finger, so put that out of your mind. I expect nothing, Marcello, and I hope for nothing more than to leave this apartment with some semblance of our old relationship still intact.'

For the longest time their gazes held, her hazel eyes repeating what her lips had just uttered, words that were exactly what he'd needed to hear. Hearing them, though, and seeing them alive in her eyes brought none of the relief he would expect, and it took a long time before he was able to control the beats of doom pounding inside him enough to suck a long breath in.

'I am sorry for making assumptions,' he said heavily. 'I haven't been with a virgin since I was one myself.'

That it had felt like it was his first time with Victoria only added to the weight of doom inside him.

'It really wasn't a big deal for me, Marcello, so please don't make it one for you.'

How could he not make it a big deal when he had so many contrasting emotions thrashing through him? The most unwelcome of them all was the secret thrill that kept punching through the acridity. He'd been Victoria's first. She'd given herself to *him*.

Damn it all to hell, how was he supposed to make sense of any of this?

'I mean it,' she said into the silence, peering at him intently, reading him better than anyone else in the world. 'My virginity is irrelevant.'

'Was,' he supplied tautly.

'What?'

'*Was* irrelevant. It is gone. Given to a man who didn't deserve it when there must be hundreds—thousands—

of men out there who would be able to give you everything you wish for.'

Her eyes narrowed. 'My virginity wasn't a prize to give, thank you very much, and how do you know what I wish for?'

'You come from a big family. Do you not want that for yourself?'

'I want a family of my own but not yet. Not for a long time.'

But she did want one. In his heart, he'd always known it, had recognised it in the softening of her stare at Denise's baby.

'Then why did you hold on to it for so long?'

'It wasn't a case of holding out. It's just the way life worked out for me.'

He couldn't stop himself asking, 'How?'

Her shrug was almost imperceptible. 'I'm the plainest of five sisters and from a town so small it should really be called a glorified village. There were hardly any boys there and the ones who weren't gay all fancied one or other of my sisters. They never gave me a second glance. Not a single boy asked me out until I arrived in America.'

'Are Irish boys all blind?' he asked incredulously. How anyone could consider Victoria plain was beyond all comprehension. That she should consider herself plain…he made a mental note to drag her to an optician at the soonest opportunity.

Her beautiful features relaxed and she gave a soft

laugh. 'My sisters are all stunning. I know I'm not ugly but compared to them I'm nothing. When I started at Columbia, I had hopes of finding a nice boy, but I swear American boys are a different breed from Irish ones—they were all so *confident*, and because I was this duck out of water trying to find her feet in a strange country, I ran a mile from them. By the time I graduated, I'd loosened up a bit but all the decent ones had paired off, and then I started at Hansons and, as you know, it's run and staffed by cretins, and then I was poached by this gorgeous Italian man to work as his executive assistant and any hope of finding someone went out of the window by the constant demands he made on my time outside working hours.'

Something stuck in his throat at the same moment something relaxed in him, just as he'd just seen Victoria visibly relax.

He *was* making too much of her virginity. He was making too much of this whole thing. He'd crossed a Rubicon he'd sworn never to cross and made love to his closest employee, and there was no turning back. What was done was done. He could spend the rest of the night castigating himself for something that couldn't be reversed or…

'This Italian man…' He leaned his face close to hers. 'He sounds like a monster.'

She held his stare a long moment before her lips curved into a smile.

'He is,' she promised solemnly. 'He has no concept

of personal time. I've lost count of the times he's woken me in the middle of the night because he needs something and doesn't want to wake his household staff, and that's not forgetting the time he basically bullied me away from a theatre show I'd spent months looking forward to seeing for the sake of finding a Montblanc pen.'

He ran a finger down her delicate jawline. 'Definitely a monster. How do you put up with him?'

'By putting his photo on a board and throwing darts at it whenever I have a minute to myself, and by dreaming up inventive ways to maim him.'

The darkness curdling inside him finally lifted as laughter broke free, lifting and floating away completely when the widest smile lit Victoria's face, a moment that felt so good and right that he stamped on the voice warning him strongly against taking her into his arms again, and hauled her back to him. The moment her laughing mouth fused with his, the voice evaporated.

CHAPTER EIGHT

VICTORIA OPENED HER eyes to find Marcello holding a bulging paper bag. The hugest, smuggest smile was on his face.

'Bagels?' she guessed sleepily.

'And coffee. Sit up, breakfast is served.'

Covering a yawn, she held the duvet to her naked breasts and propped her back against the velvet headboard.

'Bacon, cream cheese and avocado,' he said, handing her a wrapped bagel with a flourish.

She blinked her surprise.

He grinned and swooped a kiss on her mouth. 'My powers of observation are limitless.'

'And only slightly lesser than your ego.'

'Impossible.'

Laughing, she unwrapped the still-warm goodie in her hands and took a bite. After days of her only sustenance coming from Marcello's attempts at cooking, it tasted like heaven. That Marcello had ordered it—his plain T-shirt, low-slung shorts and bare feet suggested he hadn't left the apartment to buy them—and that he'd ordered her favourite fillings only made it sweeter. When he stripped those few items and climbed into bed, she thought it might be the single happiest moment of her life.

The talk they'd had after their first time had helped settle Victoria's mind. She'd gone into this with her eyes wide open and she would not close them to reality now. She would take this time with Marcello for exactly what it was: a short but very sweet affair. She would hide away the emotions and think only of the pleasure for as long as it lasted.

'Does this mean Manhattan's back in business?' she asked between bites.

He swallowed the last of his first bagel and dug into the bag for another. 'The bagel shop is.'

'Priorities, eh?'

He winked and took a huge bite of his second bagel. She wasn't in the least surprised when he unwrapped a third for himself or, when she couldn't eat the third one he'd brought for her, that he devoured it too. The meal he'd been going to cook before the power cut had been forgotten by them both. All they'd been hungry for was each other.

'So?' she prompted, determinedly keeping her voice chirpy. 'Is Manhattan back in business?' Meaning, is the Guardiola Group reopening its New York doors?

He shook his head. 'It is still treacherous out there. There are thirty-foot snowdrifts trapping people in their homes, thousands of cars buried… I have given the order to continue working from home until Monday.' He brushed his mouth to her ear, sending delicious shivers lacing her spine. 'It is far too unsafe for you to return to your apartment. You will have to stay here for days longer.'

The purest relief filled her chest.

Days longer to enjoy the bliss of Marcello without the real world intruding.

Eyes gleaming lasciviously, he had a drink of his coffee.

'What?' she asked, noticing the funny way he was staring at her.

He shook his head before his perfect teeth flashed. 'Your hair.'

She put a hand to it. 'What's wrong with it?'

'It looks like a bird's nest.'

'That's because *someone* made mad, passionate love to me while it was still wet from the bath.' And then made love to her again before insisting she get some sleep, only to wake her when daylight filtered into the bedroom for more lovemaking.

It had been the best night of her life and she would cherish the memories for the rest of her life, and make the most of the memories as they made them because it wouldn't be long until the rest of her life opened up. When they next stepped into the skyscraper that homed the Guardiola Group, this brief affair would be over, something they both understood without either having to put it into words.

It couldn't be any other way.

Whether their working relationship could survive it, only time would tell. For now, all she wanted was to live for the moment.

His blue eyes glittered. 'Not that Italian monster you spoke of?'

'I'm afraid so.'

Eyes not leaving her face, he put his coffee cup on the bedside table, then plucked her cup out of her hand and put it down too. The paper bag filled with their wrappings and napkins he threw onto the floor.

Pinching the top of the duvet, Marcello slowly pulled it down, exposing all of Victoria's curvaceous body to his greedy eyes. Bagel crumbs had nestled on the top of her breasts and he dipped his head to lick them off, thrilling at her shivers.

'The Italian monster you speak of needs to make penance,' he murmured as he circled a large, rosy nipple with his tongue.

Her back arched. Fingers laced through his hair. 'Oh?'

Still lavishing attention on her beautifully weighty breasts, he trailed a finger down her rounded belly to her pubis. 'The monster will be your slave for pleasure,' he whispered seductively, sliding a finger inside her and thrilling to find her already hot and sticky for him.

She moaned. 'My slave…?' Her voice broke as he rubbed his thumb over her bud.

'Your slave. Here to cater to all your desires.' Raising his face to hers, he gently bit her bottom lip and increased the friction of his thumb. 'Tell me your desires and fantasies, *bella*. All of them.'

'Just…' She moaned again and writhed into his hand. 'Just…just keep doing that.'

Being Victoria Cusack's sex slave was, Marcello decided a few mornings later whilst trying to catch his breath in her arms, a very fulfilling occupation. She was proving to be an exacting, insatiable mistress, growing bolder with her demands the longer time passed.

The sex between them was out of this world. So incredible was it that he refused to think about the real world that was waiting for them. His household staff were all back and working and had been given strict instructions to keep out of his bedroom. He'd ordered his finance director to run the Guardiola empire in his absence, and given strict company-wide instructions that he wasn't to be disturbed unless a matter of life or death cropped up.

For the first time in over a decade, he forgot about work altogether and lived for the moment… Which was why it came as a shock when a message pinged into his phone from one of only a handful of numbers he'd set to override his phone being on silent.

Cursing to himself, he rolled off Victoria's heavenly body to read it.

She rolled with him and kissed his shoulder blade. 'Is there a problem?'

'It is a message from Benito.'

'Your brother?'

His brother and also the head of the European side of Marcello's empire. 'He has questions about the keynote speech I agreed to make.'

Victoria's lips stilled against his skin. He knew without having to ask that the real world had just penetrated her as it had him.

'That's only a week away.'

'Sì,' he agreed heavily. They were scheduled to leave next Friday for it.

'You should call him back.'

'Later.' Firing a message to his brother saying just that, he put his phone down and turned onto his back. Immediately, Victoria slung her arm over his waist and cuddled into him.

'Everything's already organised for the conference, and all the travel to and from it,' she told him quietly.

He kissed the top of her head. 'I know.' Victoria would have organised everything with her usual forensic efficiency.

He still couldn't understand why he'd agreed to it. Marcello avoided Rome as much as possible. It had been during his latest Christmas visit, over a game of pool in their parents' games room, that Benito had asked Marcello to make the keynote speech at a conference he was organising. He didn't know which of them had been more surprised at his acceptance.

He'd called Victoria straight away to inform her. He remembered the noise in the background. She'd been playing charades with her family. There had been a huge smile in her voice. He'd suspected she might have been a little tipsy, something that had made *him* smile.

'I've done the first draft of the speech for you too.'

He kissed her again and held his mouth to the hair he'd combed conditioner through when they'd shared a bath. Victoria was the only person he'd ever trusted to write a speech for him. She had an unerring ability to put herself in his head and write as if she were speaking from his mouth. He rarely made alterations to them.

Damn it, he couldn't lose her.

It was impossible that they could return to the status quo of their working life but he had to find a way to ensure this affair between them didn't have the repercussions he'd feared before it had even started. He would do whatever it took to keep her by his side as his right-hand woman. Whatever was necessary.

'Let's take a walk into Central Park,' he impulsively suggested. Get some fresh air into their lungs and into his head. Prove to himself that he could go more than a few hours without having to make love to her.

She lifted her head and rested her chin on his chest, bemused doubt in her stare. 'You? Walk?'

'Why not? We only have two days left before we return to the office.'

There was a flicker in her eyes but her bemused smile didn't falter. 'Are you seriously telling me you have suitable clothes to go trekking through feet-high snow in?'

'All the roads and paths have been cleared.'

'You wear handstitched shoes. They will be ruined.'

'I am sure there is an outdoor clothing shop that will deliver stuff to me…' A thought occurred to him, a thought that was, to his mind, a most excellent idea.

'What?' she asked.

He smiled. Truly, no one knew him or could read him better than Victoria Cusack. 'I have just thought of the perfect surprise for my favourite redhead.'

'Which is?'

'It will not be a surprise if I tell you, will it?'

'Please?'

'No.'

Her fingers slid down his abdomen and she kissed his nipple. 'Please?'

He sprang to immediate attention. 'No.'

Wrapping her fingers around his arousal, she gripped it with just the right pressure and lazily moved her hand up and down the shaft. 'Please?'

'No.'

Keeping hold of him, she lifted herself so her face was over his. Still masturbating him, she hooked her thigh between his legs and kissed him deeply, parting his lips with her tongue and moaning into his mouth.

Threading his fingers into her hair, Marcello closed his eyes and submitted to the eroticism of Victoria's hand pleasuring him, her pubis grinding into his thigh, the weight of her breasts pressed against his skin, and her hot mouth devouring him.

'Please?' she breathed into his ear, now masturbating him with the vigour he craved.

'You are not playing fair,' he groaned.

'I know.' And with that, she released his arousal and twisted around so her back was to him.

'Why, you little tease…' Moving quicker than he'd done since childhood, he ignored her kicks and squeals of laughter as he tussled with her and pinned her onto her back.

They were both still laughing when, fully sheathed, he drove himself inside her.

Victoria thought the best thing about being a billionaire had to be the way it made mere mortals bow to your requests. Two hours after Marcello suggested a walk in Central Park, they were both dressed for an Arctic expedition and crossing the slushy, gritted road, heading towards the most magical of winter wonderlands. Fresh snow had settled overnight and covered it all afresh, and it seemed that the whole of Manhattan had come out to experience it, families building snowmen, children being pulled along on sleds by hardy parents, even hardier joggers making the most of their freedom and ploughing their own trail.

'Shall we skate?' he suggested when they spotted an ice rink through the trees ahead.

'I don't know how.'

'Then I shall teach you.'

'You know how to skate?' she asked, amazed.

'My grandparents lived in Milan near the Bagni Misteriosi. It is the most beautiful outdoor swimming pool and in the winter it is turned into an ice rink. When we were children, Benito and I spent much of our Christmas holidays skating on it.'

Once upon a time, Victoria would have changed the subject at such a personal turn to a conversation. It had been a part of the rhythm of their lives. Talk about anything and everything so long as it didn't have real meaning. Now, though, everything was different. She was different. They were different. And it was his use of the past tense that made her carefully ask, 'Are they still with us?'

'My grandfather is. He moved back to Rome after my grandmother died. That was a few months before I poached you.'

'Oh, I'm sorry. I didn't know.'

Victoria had met his parents during their last two visits to Manhattan and thought them lovely, warm people. She wouldn't have guessed they'd been suffering a recent bereavement.

He squeezed her hand. 'No need to be sorry. She was very ill and now she is at peace.'

They'd reached the queue waiting their turn on the rink.

'Shall we?' he invited.

'You're sure you can teach me?'

He raised his eyebrows. 'You doubt me?'

Laughing, she shook her head. 'If I know you, you were probably good enough to turn professional.'

'It was suggested,' he said without an ounce of fake modesty that only made her laugh harder.

'What stopped you?'

'It was a winter hobby. I cannot help that I am naturally talented at everything.'

She'd only just stopped the tears rolling down her cheeks when he used his magic charm to wangle them to the front of the queue without a pre-booked ticket, and without anyone trying to kill them.

Marcello could not remember a better day. Watching Victoria attempt to ice skate would go down in his annals of history. If he lived to be a hundred he would never forget the day his super-professional right-hand woman was laughed at by small children zooming past her. If he lived to be one hundred he would never forget his pride at the moment she finally dared let go of his hand and skated three feet on her own. Afterwards, they'd shared a giant box of churros dipped in chocolate and drank mulled wine, then taken a carriage ride back to his apartment with the sun setting behind them. Her joy at this had lit her face into something that transcended beauty.

The best part came when they returned to his apartment and she found a pile of boxes laid on the freshly laundered and made bed.

The large hazel eyes landed on him with a question. He adored that her cheeks were still rosy from the cold.

He sat on the armchair. 'Open the Genevieve box first.'

Excitement thrumming—Genevieve was the current go-to designer of New York's elite—Victoria removed the lid and carefully parted the tissue paper to lift out a red velvet dress. Shaking it out, she fingered the soft texture with amazement then looked back at Marcello. Expectation was alive on his face.

'This is for me?'

'Unless you know another Victoria who wears the same size dress as you. Take another look in the box.'

At the bottom lay an envelope with her name on it. Her heart thumping, she opened it and gasped to find two tickets to the Broadway show she'd abandoned Sheena at. Peering closer, she saw they were for the next night and in what had to be the centre front of the mezzanine.

'I have been assured that they are the best seats possible for this show,' he said. 'We will be able to see the whole ensemble perform without any restrictions, and the acoustics are supposed to be incredible.'

She just gaped at him.

'I can easily change them for orchestra seating if you would prefer?'

And he would. She saw that. The Lord alone knew how he'd managed to get these spectacular seats at this short notice—she imagined a large amount of money had been exchanged in bribes and sweeteners—and the royal *we* he'd used…

Marcello would be going with her. Marcello who, when she'd first told him she was going to watch this particular musical, had asked why on earth she wanted to waste hours watching people prance around singing and dancing on stage dressed as witches.

And now he would be taking her.

This was his surprise for her and just as he'd used sweeteners to procure the tickets, the show itself was a sweetener. His last gift before he said goodbye to her as a lover.

'Do you want me to change them?' he asked, doubt creasing his forehead.

She swallowed to loosen her throat, and shook her head. 'These are perfect, thank you. And so is the dress.'

The doubt remained. 'You are sure?'

Not wanting to spoil what for Marcello was the most thoughtful and unselfish gift he could have given her, she smiled through the pain lacing her veins. 'When I went with Sheena, we were so far back in the gods that the cast were like ants.'

The crease in his forehead changed. 'Sheena?'

'My old roommate.'

Understanding dawned. 'You went to see the show with a girl friend?'

She nodded.

To her amazement, he burst out laughing. The sound rumbled through the vast bedroom and soothed her despondency enough for her to straddle his lap and rest her hands on his chest.

'What's so funny?'

His grin was as wide as she'd ever seen it. 'I thought you had gone on a real date.'

'That's what I wanted you to think.' Leaning her face into his, she eyeballed him and added, 'I stupidly thought you'd give me some peace for the night if you thought it was a proper date.'

His hand slipped under her jumper and flattened against her naked back. 'You should have told me the truth. If I had known you were with *Sheena*, I would have waited until the next day to get you to help me find that pen.'

Her mouth dropped open. 'You sabotaged my night out on purpose?'

'Sì,' he agreed without an ounce of shame. 'I didn't want you doing what Denise did to me.'

'That's a blatant abuse of power. There are laws against things like that, you know.'

He slid his hand around and cupped her breast. Voice thickening, he said, 'We have already established that I am a monster and that monsters need to perform penance.'

Capturing the hand on her breast and squeezing it, Victoria shifted herself forward so his hardness pressed between her legs. She ground down on him. There it was. That dilation in his eyes. She would never, ever get enough of seeing that and knowing she was the reason for it, not even if they had all the time in the world…

The despondency at what the dress and theatre tickets represented suddenly lifted.

Marcello had feelings for her. She knew it as well as she knew him. He'd deliberately sabotaged what he thought was a real date. Not even he usually stooped that low: he didn't have to. It was a rare member of his vast staff who left for pastures new. Denise leaving had been an anomaly. From the few conversations Victoria had had with her predecessor, Marcello hadn't been a fraction as demanding of her personal time as he was of Victoria's.

Her chest contracted and then bloomed open, and, though she tried her best to temper it, hope rushed to fill the gap.

Frightened at the direction of her thoughts and feelings, Victoria yanked her jumper off and then kissed him hard, infusing her senses with his dark taste and driving out everything else. Dragging at his bottom lip with her teeth, she huskily whispered, 'Sabotage means serious penance.'

Marcello cupped the back of her head and pulled her mouth back to his. 'Punish me however you see fit,' he said between savage kisses.

Hazel eyes flashing their desire, she tugged at his sweater. Between them they lifted it off him before she slipped an arm behind her back and released her bra. Beautiful, bountiful breasts jutted before him, and he took one into his mouth and sucked greedily, his hands already working on the button and zip of her jeans.

With the barrier of two sets of denim between them, Marcello clasped her bottom and got to his feet, carrying her with him, then practically threw her onto the bed.

When he yanked her jeans and knickers down her legs, he had a brief memory of the first time he'd performed this same act. Then, he'd been determined to avoid letting his gaze focus on any aspect of Victoria's body. Now, he shamelessly soaked in every perfect inch.

How the hell was he supposed to return to their normal working life after this? he wondered for the hundredth time as he kissed her perfect toes and, working his way out of his own clothing, kissed his way up her perfect leg. Just to imagine being back in the office they shared…

His arousal grew even stronger as he inhaled the heat of her excitement at the same moment an image flashed in his mind of bending Victoria over his desk…

Burying his face between her legs, glorying in her moans and pleas, he submitted to his imagination and let it run riot into all the directions he'd expressly forbidden it from running before.

He didn't see how they could end it. Not yet. It was too soon.

But end it they must.

Somehow, he would have to find a way for them to work as they'd done before with this chemistry still blazing so brightly between them, but it was impossible to imagine catching a glimpse of Victoria absently chewing on her bottom lip and not wanting to replace her teeth with his own. Impossible to imagine sharing the back of the car or the cabin of his private jet and not having the need to pull her onto his lap, bunch her smart skirt around her waist, pull her knickers aside and thrust up into her, and as he imagined that, she arched her back and cried out loudly.

Crawling up to kiss her, he groped in his bedside table drawer for a condom with something bordering on fury. Finally grabbing hold of one, he yanked it out with such impatience that he knocked the drawer off its hinges. It fell to the floor with a loud clatter.

'Clumsy,' she breathed heavily as she snatched the foil from him and, with a growl, used her teeth to rip it open. 'On your back, slave.'

The fury abated as he did as commanded.

Heaven was Victoria rolling the condom over his arousal.

Nirvana was Victoria climbing on top of him and sinking down on his length, and as she grabbed his hands and placed them on her breasts then pressed her hands tightly into his chest, cheeks ablaze with the colour of her passion, he realised true nirvana would only come the day he entered her bare…

The thought was swept aside as the pleasure took control and the glory that was Victoria riding him with her head thrown back before she threw herself forward and, her lips entwined with his, ground herself down on him hard enough to bring them both to an earth-shattering climax.

Such was the force of Victoria's orgasm that she fell into the most delicious passion-induced coma in which her brain switched off but every nerve ending buzzed with pure post-coital bliss.

This was her favourite time, the silent moments when they lay replete in each other's arms, as close as it was possible for two humans to be.

Marcello's sigh brought her out of the coma. She sighed too, because she knew what it meant. Time to break the fusion.

With a kiss tender enough to make a grown woman cry, he climbed off the bed and padded to the bathroom.

Stretching, she sighed again and rolled onto her side. The bedside table loomed in her vision and she smiled, remembering why its drawer was on the floor, then peered over the side of the bed to see the mess it had made, smiling even wider to see the scattering of the restocked condoms he'd had delivered and…

The smile froze on her face.

For the longest time she stared at the photo that had fallen onto the floor with the rest of the drawer's contents before she plucked up the courage to pick it up.

It was a photo of a much younger Marcello in jeans and an open-necked navy shirt. He was cuddled next to a beautiful brunette wearing a long towelling robe.

They were sitting on a hospital bed together, beaming smiles on their faces. In Marcello's arms was a tiny newborn baby.

CHAPTER NINE

THE FIRST THING Marcello saw when he came back into the bedroom was Victoria, seemingly frozen, half hanging off the bed.

'What are you doing?' he asked, amused.

That brought her to life, and she scrambled back onto the bed...but not before he saw the photo fall from her fingers.

Their eyes met.

What he saw in her stare made his heart freeze.

She hugged the duvet around herself and whispered, 'I'm sorry. I didn't mean to look. I wasn't snooping, I swear.'

It took him a long moment to be able to breathe again, and even then it was through a throat that had tightened into rock.

For the first time in a decade, the past and the present collided.

His core knocked off balance and on legs that felt like they belonged to someone else, Marcello walked to the mess on the floor made by the drawer he'd knocked out, and picked up the photo. It was the original of the photo he carried in his wallet so it could always be kept close to him.

It was his most treasured possession.

It would be the easiest thing in the world to put the drawer back in place, tuck the photo back into its place inside it, and dredge up a meaningless conversation to skip over the whole thing.

If he was with anyone but Victoria he would do just that, but the starkness in her stare…the compassion and the fear…

His heart heavier than it had been for many years, he sank on the bed and reached for her hand. She shuffled closer to him and, with a quiet sigh, rested her cheek on his shoulder. He could sense her stare boring into the photo and was grateful that she didn't ask any questions. Grateful for the space she gave for him to compose his thoughts.

He cleared his throat and placed a kiss into her hair. 'You have not done anything wrong so there is no need to apologise.'

Finally she spoke. Whispered. 'You're a father?'

He expelled a long breath and closed his eyes. 'Yes.'

He could hear her breathing. Could hear the questions whirling in her head.

Releasing her hand, he lightly touched his son's face. 'This is my son, Tommaso. He was born eleven years, three months and two days ago. He died when he was three days old.'

Although her heart had already known the child had

passed away, Victoria still covered her mouth to stop her horror escaping.

'He had what is known as newborn meningitis. They believe it was caused by a bacteria he caught from Livia during the birth. Completely harmless to the mother but to the newborn child…' His shoulder rose against her cheek. 'The first symptoms developed ten or so hours after this picture was taken. He did not want to wake to feed. From there…' His shoulder rose again, his accent becoming more pronounced. 'He went downhill very quickly. They did everything they could for him but he was too little. Too vulnerable. His immune system was not strong enough.'

Hot tears swimming, Victoria swallowed them back as hard and as silently as she could, utterly devastated for Marcello's loss and wretched that her curiosity over a photograph fallen on the floor had compelled him to relate what must be the most soul-wrenching period of his life.

And she'd had no idea. She didn't think anyone in America had.

He'd carried this loss for all these years…

The tears finally choked her and spilled out in a flood.

Marcello felt the heave of Victoria's sobs and, fighting back the burn in his eyes, wrapped his arms around her. Holding her tight, he kissed the top of her head and breathed in the scent of her shampoo.

'I'm sorry,' she wept into his chest, her fingers digging and clinging into his side. 'So sorry. He was so beautiful and perfect and… God, Marcello, I'm so sorry.'

'It is okay,' he whispered. It had been many years since he'd told anyone about his son. Anyone who mattered had been there at the time and had grieved with them.

Victoria mattered. Mattered far more than she should. Than he should allow.

That she should feel it so deeply…

He closed his eyes again to his own tears and breathed in more of her soothing scent.

She disentangled herself from his hold and stared at him with tears still falling over her blotchy face. 'You shouldn't be having to comfort *me*.'

He brushed a tear away with his thumb. 'The death of any child is never easy to hear about.' He wiped another tear with a sad smile and pressed a kiss to her forehead before reaching over for the box of tissues on the bedside table. He thrust them under her nose. With a grateful smile, she grabbed a handful and blew her nose while Marcello climbed off the bed and headed to the bureau he kept a bottle of his preferred eighteen-year-old single malt in. Taking the bottle and two crystal glasses, he re-joined her on the bed and poured them both a glass.

Visibly calmer, she took a small sip of hers then fixed her red-rimmed eyes back on him. 'I'm sorry you felt boxed in and compelled to tell me.'

'I'm not.'

Her eyebrows drew together.

'You *should* know that about me.' They were far beyond keeping things from each other. Their time together as lovers was coming to an end but Victoria was the most important person in his life. The last few days had taught him that much. He could envisage a future where they were both old and wrinkled and she would walk to his car with the aid of a stick and climb in next to him, and the pair of them would wheezily laugh together over the latest of life's absurdities.

She deserved to know the truth about why that future could only be as friends.

She took another drink of her whisky and, her eyes on his, held a long breath before slowly letting it out. 'Is Tommaso the reason you came to America?'

He inclined his head and drained his glass. Filling it back up, he explained, 'When Livia fell pregnant we had been having problems. The pregnancy pulled us back together and papered over the cracks in our marriage, but Tommaso's death broke us, as people and as a couple. We tried… God knows, we tried, but we could not find a way through. Not together. The old problems came back and magnified—I worked too hard, she preferred being with her sister and her mother to me. We argued over everything. Silly things. If I said something was blue she would say it was green, if she said it was pink I would insist it was black.'

He took a long sip and swirled the whisky in his mouth before swallowing it.

What he was about to say was the hardest thing to

admit to. 'I wanted out. I wanted to escape it all. We had both built a whole life in our minds of us and Tommaso, and it was taken from us, and the reminders were everywhere. Every street I walked, I had pictured walking it with him, holding his hand.

'I wanted a fresh start, not to forget him because that would be a betrayal of his life, but to breathe again. I was suffocating. Manhattan was the perfect place to relocate to. I had always enjoyed my time there and the cut and thrust of doing business there, and it was big enough and busy enough for me to immerse myself into a brand-new life. Livia did not want to come with me and I didn't try hard to convince her. We both knew we were over.'

'That's just so incredibly sad,' she said softly.

'It is,' he agreed. 'But it was the only way I could live with it. We managed to part as friends and if I am proud of anything, it is that. Livia is a wonderful woman but we were never right for each other. She has a family now with a husband who *is* right for her, and she is happy, and I built the new life I wanted for myself and have found a different kind of happiness.' He raised his glass with a wry smile. 'Even if it is happiness of a shallower kind.'

She raised a wry smile of her own. 'You came to Manhattan and conquered all before you.'

'I would trade every dollar to have my son back.' Trade his very soul.

Tears filling her eyes again, she nodded to convey that she understood.

Taking the glass from her hand, he placed it with his glass and the bottle on the bedside table then ran his fingers through her glorious hair. Strangely, the weight that had formed to see Victoria with the photo of his precious boy had lifted.

'Do not cry any more, *bella,*' he urged. 'The past cannot be changed. I have had to learn to live without him and I take each day as it comes because life is too fragile and uncertain to do anything else. Live for the moment and let the moment be this.'

Victoria parted her lips to Marcello's gently probing mouth and wound her arms around his neck, deepening the kiss, deepening the connection.

Even as she responded to his lovemaking she had to fight more tears.

Any hopes of even a tentative future with him had been dashed before they'd had the chance to fully form.

Marcello's demons went far beyond a marriage turned sour.

Grief had broken his heart beyond repair.

Somehow she would have to find a way through her own, different, grief because the physical pain of hearing his story had brought the truth home to her.

She'd fallen completely and irrevocably in love with him.

The first thing Victoria did when she woke the next morning was look out of the bedroom window. There had been another flurry of snow overnight but nothing to write home about. Nothing that promised another shutdown of Manhattan.

This time tomorrow, they would be in their office on the sixtieth floor of the skyscraper the Guardiola Group occupied, preparing for the scheduled board meeting.

Their short but beautifully hedonistic and sweet affair would be over.

She couldn't even begin to think about how she was going to cope.

Slipping her arms into Marcello's robe, she set off to find him.

She didn't have far to go. Her early bird was in his home office answering emails, wearing only a pair of boxer shorts.

His face turned to hers and lit into the dazzling smile he always greeted her with. She'd never noticed how heartbreaking it was before.

Pulling her onto his lap, he kissed her deeply, hands already breaking through the sash of the robe to roam over her body.

'*Dio*, I thought you would never wake up,' he murmured, burying his face between her breasts and manipulating her so she straddled him. His hardness pressed right at the centre point of her own arousal, feeding a hunger that had sprung from nothing but his first touch. If he didn't have the barrier of his boxers, he'd be inside her already.

'Did you bring a condom?' he asked with a groan, sucking deeply on her nipple and thrusting upwards.

Holding his head to keep him exactly where he was, rocking against him, she managed to gasp a, 'No…' at the exact moment movement from the main living area below caught her attention.

In utter horror, Victoria watched a member of the cleaning crew drag a vacuum cleaner across the room, but it took seconds before what her eyes were seeing connected with her body, and she scrambled off his lap, frantically tying the robe back together to cover her nakedness.

Marcello followed Victoria's flame-faced stare, laughed a curse and muttered, 'I need to buy a new apartment.'

Oblivious to what she'd disturbed on the overhang above her, the cleaner plugged the vacuum in just as Christina joined her from the kitchen door. She, too, was oblivious to them. That didn't stop Victoria shrinking even further back.

'They wouldn't have seen us,' he assured her.

'Yes, they would. Your balustrade is glass.'

'Tempered glass,' he corrected.

'Well, that makes all the difference.'

Amused at her unnecessary embarrassment, he reached for her hand. She dodged out of his reach.

'I don't want Christina to see me like this,' she hissed.

'Like what?'

She patted the robe. 'Like *this*.'

'Victoria, you spoke to her just last night.' The two

women had had a long discussion about their respective illnesses.

'I was wearing my own clothes then—'

'Clothes she laundered for you,' he pointed out.

'Because she knows I've been ill!'

'She knows we are currently lovers.'

If he'd thought she was embarrassed before, that was nothing to the colour her face turned now.

'She's not blind, *bella*.' Or deaf, something he failed to add in case Victoria took it on herself to dive out of the window and into the snowdrift still piled high against the side of the building to cool her flaming face off in.

'That doesn't mean I want her to see me wearing your robe!' she spluttered, before turning on her bare heel and fleeing back to the bedroom.

Following her, Marcello closed the door firmly behind him. 'There,' he said. 'Now no one can see or disturb us.'

'How do you live like this?' she asked, shaking her head with bewilderment.

'It has never been a problem before.' And it never would be again. The few women he'd allowed to stay the whole night before Victoria had been dispatched back to their own homes first thing in the morning. He could not even imagine allowing them to do that much in the future.

Coldness filled his chest to imagine allowing another woman into his bedroom at all.

It was the intensity of what he and Victoria were sharing, he assured himself as he shook off the unsettling feeling. The closeness. Opening up to her about his son and his marriage.

He stepped to her and ran his finger in the dip where the robe joined together from her neck to her cleavage. Then he pulled it apart, exposing her to him. 'Where were we?'

Victoria sat at the desk Marcello had long ago designated as hers in his home office and, for the first time in—how long? A week…? Time had flown—turned on the desktop he'd also long ago designated as hers, and opened her emails. Over four hundred new messages.

The cleaning staff had all gone. Christina and Patrick were in their own quarters. The only person who was going to disturb her was Marcello and he'd fallen asleep. She was taking no chances though, and had put her jeans and vest top on. A quick glance in the mirror had made her put her bra on too.

Back to the real office tomorrow. Back to the real world.

The real world had already found its way back to her though, and she stared at her mammoth inbox without seeing.

She'd been too caught up in the bliss of everything she was experiencing to realise Christina had figured out that they'd become lovers, and it made her cheeks burn with humiliation to imagine what the older woman must think of her. Made them burn harder to imagine what it would be like dealing with her in the future.

She knew Marcello wasn't any more ready than she was to say goodbye as lovers yet, but the unspoken deadline of their return to the office marking the end of them would not change.

The grief that had brought Marcello to Manhattan had cut too deep for him to ever dare open his heart in the same way again. He'd let her in as much as he could and tomorrow he would let her go. For him, life would return to how he needed it to be.

She'd let him so far into her heart that he'd nestled inside it with no means of release.

She closed her eyes to the swelling tears and took a long breath.

How long until he re-joined his usual dating pool? She no longer believed he would ask her to keep evenings free for him or do any of the old stuff he used to do when he had a lover on the scene—she might tease him for being a monster but he wasn't. Marcello was often thoughtless but he was never cruel—but the tabloids took a keen interest in his sex life. His shallow lovers saw to that, many using their affair as a springboard to craved fame. Victoria would once again find herself reading about his sexploits and fielding calls from disgruntled women cast aside without a thought, and know that they'd shared the bed she'd found such joy in.

All the things she'd known lay in her future and known would hurt her…

And now she knew she could not endure any of it. Because she hadn't known just how deeply in love with him she would fall.

Putting a hand to her pounding heart, she took another deep breath and blinked away the tears until she could see more clearly.

She knew what she needed to do.

Another deep breath and then she composed an email to the head of HR. She would send it in the morning, after she'd told Marcello that it would be impossible for her to go back to how things used to be.

Marcello straightened his black bow tie, flicked a speck of dust off the lapel of his black dinner jacket, then patted cologne into his shaven cheeks and neck. He was ready.

In the bedroom, Victoria stood before the full-length mirror putting on the diamond teardrop earrings he'd had delivered as a surprise for her only an hour before. If he hadn't wasted an hour of the day sleeping, he'd have snuck out and chosen them from the real-life versions and not the online versions.

He still struggled to believe he'd fallen asleep in the afternoon. His mother still regaled family and friends with stories of how, even as a toddler, Marcello had refused to nap. Since moving to Manhattan, his body's need for sleep had diminished to such an extent that he rarely slept more than five hours a night. He could only assume the copious amount of sex he'd been enjoying with Victoria was the cause of his unintended snooze. He'd woken from it, rolled over to cuddle into her and coax her into more lovemaking, only to find the bed empty. She'd returned to the room inconveniently clothed before he could seek her out. Her face had coloured when she'd explained that she'd been sorting out work stuff.

'Never mind that,' he'd said thickly, throwing off the duvet. 'Come back to bed.'

And so she had, and this time she'd been the one to doze off afterwards. When she'd woken, she'd been the one to instigate more lovemaking.

Just as he struggled to believe he'd had an afternoon snooze, he struggled to understand why his mind kept substituting the word sex for lovemaking. And why his mind flatly refused to imagine a time without Victoria in his bed.

Tomorrow they would part as lovers and return to the rhythms of their old working lives. There would be a period of adjustment but he was confident they would get through it. He was sure that throwing himself back into his pool of shallow vipers would take off the edge of his craving for his executive assistant. He would just have to be discreet, and throw himself back into the pool away from his apartment until Victoria's imprint had faded to nothing.

Back to the bland, vaguely satisfactory couplings that demanded nothing of him but his body.

Damn it, if he could keep this affair with Victoria

going until it was naturally spent then he would, but this was as much as he could allow, and he had to think, too, of what it would be like for her if they did continue things a little longer. Offices could be febrile places filled with gossip and innuendo. He would not have her humiliated. He needed her as his assistant. Needed her in his life.

His hopes for them to be old and wrinkled and wheezing together would never die. Maybe he should add the grandchildren she would surely have to the mix. Imagine them pushing the pair of them around in wheelchairs.

But where would her future husband be? he wondered, his mood dipping. To have grandchildren, she would need children first, and it was inconceivable that Victoria would choose to have children without a man by her side. A husband. A man she would pledge her life to.

His guts filled with acid.

He could provide a crèche and childcare staff in the office so she could bring her imaginary future children to work, but what if she met the father on one of her visits home and decided to move back to Ireland for real, and not just as a threat to Marcello to pull him back a peg?

She caught his stare in the mirror's reflection.

After the longest time passed, she smiled. 'You look beautiful.'

Pulling himself together, he straightened and strode over to her.

They still had this one last night together.

'Beautiful?' he said, feigning outrage. 'I think the word you are looking for is handsome.'

She turned around and gently tugged at his bow tie. Eyes on his, she said with simple sincerity, 'No. The word is beautiful.'

Her words touched something in him that made him close his eyes before taking a step back so he could drink the whole of her in. The red velvet dress fitted as if it had been tailored especially for her. Long sleeved, it dipped in a V to her breasts, giving the most tantalising glimpse of her generous cleavage, then hugged her curvy waist before cascading like drapes to her feet. Only the heels of the black knee-high boots she was wearing, a sop to the wintry weather, stopped the hem trailing on the ground. Her red hair, the perfect complementary shade to the colour of the dress, had been parted in the centre but then gathered together to fall over her right shoulder. It gleamed like the finest gold. 'No. You're the beautiful one.'

Rosy colour flushed her cheeks. 'It's the expensive makeup you bought me.'

Expensive makeup subtly but strikingly applied. 'It only enhances what God has blessed you with. You are a beautiful woman, Victoria Cusack.'

The flush deepened. 'I keep telling you, you should see my sisters. They really are beautiful. No enhancement needed,' she quipped.

He captured her chin and rubbed his thumb over the

faint cleft in it. 'Stop comparing yourself to your sisters. You are perfect exactly as you are.'

The hazel eyes softened. 'You mean that, don't you?'

He brushed a kiss over her lips and breathed her in. 'Yes. And it is time you started believing it.'

CHAPTER TEN

VICTORIA WAS SPELLBOUND. When she'd watched this musical all those months ago, her vision had been obscured and she'd been sat so high up and so far back the cast really had seemed as small as ants. She'd also kept her phone clutched in her hand, surreptitiously checking it every five minutes. When Marcello had asked her back to the office, she'd told herself she was furious with him for calling her away on something so whimsical, but now she could admit the truth to herself—she'd been waiting for it. Hoping for it. By the time her phone had silently vibrated with his call, she'd already planned her escape route to take it without disturbing the other theatregoers.

This time, she kept her phone in the gold clutch bag that had been in another of the gold boxes Marcello had surprised her with, and watched on a seat so good it was as if she could reach out and touch the stage. Maybe if her hand weren't so tightly clasped in Marcello's she would have tried.

To Marcello's surprise, he thoroughly enjoyed the show. Victoria's joy would have made it worthwhile for its own sake, but the songs were catchy and the plot good enough to keep his interest.

When things had settled between them and they'd slipped back into the old rhythm of their lives, he would take her to another Broadway show. They would go as the friends they'd been from the start. He knew it would take time to find that old rhythm but they would find it. They had to.

But not yet. Tonight they were enjoying Broadway as lovers.

Outside, the snow was falling again, and when they climbed into the back of his waiting car for the short drive to the restaurant he'd booked them to dine at, fat flakes clung like sparkling diamonds in her hair before melting into a glisten and vanishing.

Palming her cold cheek, he leaned his face into hers and thought he would never be able to endure seeing the sparkle in her eyes vanish, not when they shone with such brilliance as they did now. 'Go on, tell me, how many times have you already seen it?' he murmured.

She grinned. 'Four times. How did you guess?'

'Your singing along to every word was the giveaway.'

Both laughing, they kissed, a short kiss because their short drive had ended.

Marcello watched for a reaction when she recognised the name of the restaurant, and experienced a surge of gratification when the sparkle in her eyes intensified. Famed for its fresh atmosphere and even fresher seafood, something he knew she had a deep and abiding love for, he'd selected this place with Victoria's desires at the forefront of his mind.

Thinking there was a very real danger she could burst from happiness, Victoria felt like a celebrity when they were whisked up the steps and welcomed into what she could only describe as a sophisticatedly funky interior. Evening coats taken—her Merino wool coat had been another surprise from Marcello—they were swept off to a corner table. Water poured, drink order taken, a limoncello vodka martini for Victoria, a dirty vodka, whatever that was, for Marcello, and then they were left alone with their menus.

Immediately, she leaned her face over her menu to confide, 'I looked at bringing Sheena here for her birthday last summer but couldn't get a reservation for love nor money.' She'd been snootily informed the restaurant had a fourteen-month waiting list. 'She is going to be *green* when I tell her I've been.'

'You should have told me—I could have got the two of you in.'

'Don't *ever* tell Sheena that.' Not that he would ever meet her. Not now. Marcello didn't know it but this wasn't just their last night together. This was the beginning of their end, something she was resolutely not allowing herself to think about. He'd gone to so much effort that it would be cruel to ruin the evening by letting her emotions get the better of her. There would be plenty of time for that when she broke the news to him.

Let them have this one last night and part with the best memories of each other.

He grinned. ‘How do you know Sheena? Did you meet at Columbia?’

‘No, after Columbia. We lived together for a while. I was looking for a new place to live and she was looking for a new roommate. Mutual friends facilitated it and introduced us. They were convinced that as we’re both Irish we were bound to know each other because obviously everyone from Ireland knows each other.’

His grin widened. ‘I used to get that when I first moved here. Anyone with a first-generation Italian friend was certain we must have spent our childhoods together.’

‘Do you know what the best bit is?’

His eyes gleamed. ‘Tell me.’

‘It turned out that Sheena and I *did* kind of know each other. Our mothers used to work for the same accountancy firm!’

Oh, how she loved Marcello’s laughter at this, loved how when their drinks arrived he held his aloft so she could clink hers to it, loved how he urged her to try his and loved even more his laughter when she pulled a disgusted face—who put *olive juice* in a vodka, for heaven’s sake?—at its offensive taste.

‘Your tastebuds are warped,’ she informed him.

‘So you don’t want to share the seafood platter, then?’ he teased.

It was after they’d finished their first course, were

on their third round of drinks and helping themselves to the enormous tray heaped with clams, oysters, tuna crudo, jumbo shrimps and lobster that had been delivered to their table, that he said, 'Do you know, I have never asked what brought you to America?'

She looked up at him, startled by the observation. 'Haven't you?'

He shook his head. 'I just assumed you had followed the American dream like most other people who emigrate here.'

The look that passed between them conveyed perfectly well that it didn't need to be said that Marcello had turned his back on a nightmare rather than follow a dream.

'I did have that dream,' she admitted, squeezing lemon juice over the seafood she'd piled onto her plate. 'But it wasn't the dream of making a pot of money. It was the freedom New York promised that drew me.'

'What kind of freedom were you seeking?'

'All kinds. I'm from a small town with a small high street where all the shops close at five and the only night life are pubs where the only activities are games of darts and table skittles, and the music comes from twenty-year-old jukeboxes. New York seemed to promise everything I thought I was missing out on. The city that never sleeps? I wanted that, thank you very much.'

Marcello laughed and plucked a fat chip from the metal basket piled with them. 'That aspect drew me too. Did you not consider moving to an Irish city or to England?'

'All my favourite films were set in New York so for me it was a no-brainer. I couldn't believe it when I was accepted into Columbia. I only chose business on a whim because I couldn't think of anything else.'

'You were eighteen?'

'I'd just turned nineteen.'

He thought of himself at nineteen. He'd gone to university in Bologna, a four-hour drive from his family home in Rome. His parents had visited every other weekend armed with cases of freshly laundered clothes, which they'd swapped for the mounds of dirty clothes he'd piled all over his cramped room.

Where he'd been happily spoilt and cosseted by adoring parents, Victoria had fought to be seen by hers. Moving to New York meant Victoria had been on her own. In the eighteen months she'd worked for him, not a single member of her family had flown out to visit her.

'That must have been daunting.'

'It was *terrifying*,' she agreed gleefully.

'And your family? What did they think of you leaving? Were they proud?' He hoped as hard as he'd ever hoped for anything that they were.

'They were delighted for me. I became the golden Cusack they could all brag about to their friends and casually drop into conversation about my life in The Big Apple.' The gleefulness in her voice faded. 'It took me leaving to make them actually remember my name.'

That was one thing he would never understand. He supposed in big families like the Cusacks, it was all too easy for one of them to feel lost within it. Marcello's extended family was big, but when he was growing up, his immediate family had been just the four of them, their parents spoiling and cosseting Benito as much as they'd done him.

He found himself having to swallow a sudden lump in his throat. 'Do you miss them?'

'Not as much as I would without the technology we have. I'm in all the family group chats and stuff but…' She gave a small shrug. 'It's silly but I still feel excluded. It's my own fault, I know. I chose to move across the Atlantic and live in a different time zone from them. But they answer each other's posts within minutes, sometimes seconds whereas mine are often left hanging. The only one who always responds to mine is Grandma.'

Victoria gave a wistful shake of her head and tried to pull herself together and not let the despondency she'd worked so hard to smother that evening leach out. 'I told you I'm being silly. It's always great when I go home and we have such a lovely time together. I guess I just wish it didn't feel like they forget me the minute I'm out of their sight.'

But as she said this, she realised that since working for Marcello, the sting of it had lost its needle precision. Her visits home had been happier occasions for her, not just because she no longer felt lost in the crowd of Cusacks but because she was happier and more confident in her own skin. And all because one man had seen something in her that had left a lasting impression.

Marcello had remembered her.

'I can tell you this much, *bella*,' he said. 'When you were ill, I nearly suffered a burst eardrum from all the calls I kept receiving from them.'

She spluttered a short burst of laughter at the imagery.

His smile was soft. 'I cannot pretend to understand the dynamics of your family but I know they love you.'

She returned the smile. 'I know they do. I guess it's all a continuation of how things were for me growing up. My voice always got lost.' She wrinkled her nose. 'I probably should have shouted louder to make myself heard. That's what the others did.'

'If you did not have your voice there, I would say that you have found it here.'

'Do you think?'

'There is not a person in the Guardiola Group who would dare ignore your voice.'

'You make me sound like a dragon!'

Laughing, he shook his head and cut into his tuna. 'No one thinks that. People listen to you because you have proven that you're worth listening to. You organise your thinking the same way you organise my life.'

'Thank you… I think.'

'*Bella*, it is not just me who values and respects you. The whole workforce does.'

The tears she'd been fighting so hard to hold back suddenly brimmed as the life she'd enjoyed since arriving in New York flashed through her. The good friends she'd made. The great social life she'd enjoyed even if it had ground to a halt since working for Marcello. But that was her own fault too. She saw that now. She'd let him make outrageous demands on her personal time because, even when she was miffed with him, there was no one in the world in whose company she'd rather be.

Because of Marcello, she'd found a career to thrive in and was paid generously for it. For all that she'd often thought of herself as his glorified dogsbody, he'd taught her more about business than any number of degrees could have. He'd made it no secret that he was grooming her to one day take a seat on his board, a seat in her own right and not just as his Woman Friday.

At twenty-five, she'd built the life her bored, insecure teenage self would have thrilled for.

Tomorrow, she would take a sledgehammer to it.

Today she had everything. A great career. Disposable income. A decent apartment to live in. A love affair more fulfilling and consuming than she could ever have dreamed possible.

Tomorrow it would all be gone.

'*Bella?* What is wrong?'

She looked back into the eyes she loved more than anyone's in the whole world and knew that in the morning she would be taking a sledgehammer to Marcello's world too, even if it was a much smaller one.

But tomorrow hadn't arrived yet. They still had these

last few hours together and she wouldn't spoil them for anything.

With a soft sigh, she said, 'I was just thinking my teenage self would approve of how my life has turned out.'

Shoulders relaxing, he raised his glass. 'We should drink to that.'

'As long as I don't have to drink that evil stuff in your glass,' she managed to quip.

His answering laugh helped smother the despondency back to where she could keep it hidden and contained from them both for their last few hours together.

Marcello's eyes were wide open in the early morning darkness. He wasn't sure if he'd slept at all. Too many thoughts crowding his head in the lulls between love-making.

Nestled beside him, her hand a deadweight on his abdomen, a strand of her long hair tickling his arm, Victoria.

The dream-like bubble of the past week was coming to an end. Soon, he would have to wake her. They needed to shower and then head to her apartment so she could change into her work clothes before they went into the office and reminded the staff of what they looked like.

He hadn't had so much time off work since Tommaso.

It had been a difficult birth. Livia had suffered. But then their perfect baby had been born and happiness had suffused her. Suffused them both. The purest kind of love. The three of them, his little family. A whole life together to be lived.

In the blink of an eye it had all gone and the purity of his love had turned into a grief so unbearable the pain had made him want to die.

Work had been his salvation. He'd returned to the small building that had homed his then small empire the day after they'd laid Tommaso to rest. He'd taken only rare days off since. His annual visit to his parents' home for Christmas was always calculated to last no more than four days, including travelling. Work hard. Play hard. Exhaust the mind and body. Leave no time for thoughts or feelings.

His thoughts now refused to switch off but, without any forethought, he slipped out of bed and headed silently to his dressing room, closing the door before switching the light on so the brightness didn't wake Victoria.

Behind his rails of shirts, he unlocked the hidden safe he kept his more expensive valuables in. He didn't possess many of them. He'd never been one for status symbols. A handful of ridiculously expensive watches, a signet ring he always felt like a mafia boss wearing, a few pairs of diamond cufflinks too expensive to go into the cufflink drawer, and his grandmother's engagement ring.

'You're the only one left who can use it,' his grandfather had said when he'd given it to him over Christmas.

Meaning Marcello was the only one of his grandchildren unmarried, something his mother, who'd abandoned any subtlety of her hope that Marcello remarry this past year, had no doubt put in his mind.

If he hadn't respected his grandfather so greatly, and if he hadn't understood his well-meant intention, Marcello would have reminded him that he was unmarried because he was divorced and that the scars from what he and Livia had been through meant he would never marry again.

The ghost of Livia's voice echoed through the walls from the last time he'd seen her.

Then why did you come here?

He was still no closer to an answer. No closer, either, to understanding why he'd agreed to the keynote speech in Rome. He'd refused his brother's four previous requests so why accept this one? Why put himself through the pain of returning to the city of his darkest days when he didn't need to?

And why was he standing in his dressing room staring at a ring? He didn't know why he'd felt compelled to look at it. Didn't understand the hollowness of his mood or the brooding nature of his thoughts.

Exhaling through his nose, he locked the safe back up and moved his shirts back into place to cover it, then turned out the dressing room light and gazed at Victoria through the dim moonlight pouring through the windows. She'd turned over and huddled deeper into the duvet.

His next exhale was a fight against his own airwaves.

He'd let her sleep a little longer.

Showered, still trying to make sense of his thoughts and feelings, Marcello selected his suit, then rifled through his ties. The hot water had done him the world of good and washed away much of the strange mood that had clung to him. He'd figured out, too, what had caused it. It was all the talk and thoughts about Tommaso. The grief he usually kept compartmentalised had risen these last few days. Longer really. He'd thought about his son more in recent times than he usually ever allowed himself.

Victoria was still asleep.

He watched her from the bedroom door as he'd done a short while earlier from his dressing room, a fresh weight forming in his guts.

This would be the last time he saw her like this.

He closed his eyes and breathed out the pain.

It had to be this way.

CHAPTER ELEVEN

DREAD LAY HEAVY in Victoria from the moment consciousness pulled her from sleep.

This was it. The day she destroyed her own happiness and threw away everything she'd worked for.

Stifling a whimper, she rolled over, seeking out Marcello. His side of the bed was empty.

Cuddling into his pillow, she squeezed her eyes shut and breathed in the remnants of his scent. She wanted desperately to make love to him one last time, before she detonated the bomb. Experience the blissful closeness one last time.

His robe was slung on the back of the armchair, and she wrapped herself in it before searching for him. His office and the living space below were both empty.

She tried to draw air into her tight lungs.

The dread spread into her limbs. She had to drag her legs back to the bedroom.

With still no sign of Marcello, she took a quick shower and tried her hardest not to think of standing under this very shower only hours ago with him, when they'd returned from the restaurant. Brushed her teeth trying not to remember how, only hours ago, Marcello had stood at the adjoining sink brushing his own teeth.

Christina had laundered her clothes for her again, and when Victoria tugged her grey cashmere sweater over her head and then straightened it over her stomach, there was a beat when she thought she glimpsed the pounding of her heart pushing through her chest.

The door opened.

Marcello strode into the bedroom carrying two cups of coffee. He was already dressed for the office in a white shirt, navy trousers and a matching waistcoat.

'Good morning, Victoria,' he said in greeting, as if he were already back in the work office and had beaten her in by ten minutes. He put her coffee on the table by the armchair, and stood with his own close to the door. Already creating a distance between them. Already showing that this was the point they returned to how things should have stayed.

Her heart twisted to see his tie. Its knot was too big. Marcello was always precise with his knots.

'You are ready?' he asked.

Somehow she managed to form a nod.

He gave a sharper nod of his own. '*Bene.* The car will be here in fifteen minutes.' He flashed his heartbreaking smile. 'Bagels will be delivered momentarily.'

Bagels? In that moment, she couldn't even conjure the image of one. The world was swimming around her and it was taking every ounce of her strength to keep hold of the emotions battering her into a bruise.

She thought she might be sick.

Gripping the cup tightly, she lifted it to her lips.

There was no comfort in the warm, familiar bitter-sweetness.

His tone became even lighter. 'How did I do?'

He was unshaved, she realised with another twist of her heart. Unshaved for the office. It was a sight that made her want to cry. 'You made it?'

Another dazzling smile. It didn't meet his eyes. 'My first attempt at making coffee in a decade. Marks out of ten?'

'A definite nine,' she croaked through her splintering heart.

'It appears I am as naturally talented at making coffee as everything else,' he said with a deadpan modesty that would normally make her laugh but now made her eyes fill with tears. 'Other than cooking, that is. But do not think this means I will be taking on coffee-making duties in the office—this is strictly a one-time event.'

He continued talking as he reached for the door handle, his accent becoming more pronounced with every word. 'We will stop at your apartment on our way to the office so you can change before the board meeting. I have already—'

'Marcello, stop,' she interrupted softly, unable to bear the faux normality a second longer.

His hand tightened around the door handle but his light expression didn't change.

She shook her head whilst frantically blinking the

tears away, and tried her hardest to control her wobbling chin. 'I'm sorry but I can't do this.'

Marcello's grip on the door handle was so tight he could feel the bones of his knuckles press against his skin.

He could no longer ignore Victoria's pallor. She was paler than she'd been since her illness. More than pale.

The weight he'd woken to in his guts spread and clamped his heart in a vice.

Her eyes shining with tears, she shook her head again.

He cleared his throat. 'What can't you do?'

But he knew. His weighted guts had known it the moment their eyes had locked together when he'd come back into the bedroom with their coffee. The misery contained in her stare.

Her grip on her cup was as tight as his hold on the door handle. 'I can't go back to the office and pretend that nothing happened between us.'

'It will be difficult,' he admitted evenly, in what he knew was the understatement of the century. They'd both known it would be difficult to return to how things had been. 'But we are both professionals, and—'

'I can't go back to how we were. Not now.'

His heart was thumping so hard it was a struggle to hear his own voice over it. 'Would you like to take a few days' paid leave? That might be the best thing for both of us—a short reset and then we…'

But she was shaking her head.

A tear rolled down her cheek. 'A few days is not going to reset my feelings. I'm sorry.'

'Okay, paid leave for the week, until our trip to Rome on...'

But she was still shaking her head. More tears spilled down her distressed face. 'It can never work, Marcello. Not for me. Not now.'

'Don't be so defeatist,' he chided through the scratching in his throat and the hot pulse raging in his head as his planned route to a dotage with Victoria in his life and her grandchildren pushing them around on wheelchairs began evaporating before his eyes.

'Marcello, *please*.' Victoria put the coffee cup on the table and wiped the tears away, wishing with all her splintering heart that she could turn back time a week and a day, to the morning her phone had woken her at five a.m. Wished she could put herself back in her bed and ignore his call.

But she'd never been able to ignore him. The pull of hearing his voice or seeing a written message from him had always been too powerful to resist. Marcello had become her whole world long before she'd even realised it.

And now she had to walk away from it.

A pulse was throbbing on his unshaven jaw. 'Victoria, we will make it work as we said we would. Whatever you need to readjust, I will provide it, and then—'

'But there is no way, don't you see?' she implored. 'I can't spend twelve hours a day every day by your side feeling the way I do. I just can't. It would kill me.'

His head reared as if she'd slapped it.

'What...?' His voice trailed off, and he stared at her as if looking at her for the very first time.

As much as she wanted to turn her stare away, she forced herself to hold the lock of their eyes. Forced him to read what was in hers.

Shocked understanding flared.

He shook his head slowly, as if in disbelief.

She simply held his gaze until, without uttering a word, he staggered over to the bed and sank onto it, cradling his head in his hands.

'Now do you understand?' she whispered.

The silence was so total that when he dragged his hands down his cheeks she could hear the scratching of his fingers against the stubble.

He tilted his head back slowly. Blew out an equally slow breath.

Feeling sicker than she'd ever done in her life, Victoria sank onto her knees before him and captured his stubbly cheeks in her hands. She could feel the barely suppressed tension breathing out from his pores.

'You don't have to leave,' he said raggedly, turning his mouth into her palm. 'We can find a way to make it work.'

'The only way it can work for me is if you love me—'

His eyes squeezed shut as he let out a long groan. 'No, Victoria, don't say it.'

'But I do love you,' she told him quietly. 'I think a part of me has always loved you.'

The strong throat she loved nothing more than burying her face into and breathing in the scent from moved, but nothing came out. It made her broken heart splinter a little more to know she would never breathe in his scent again.

'Do you think I wanted this to happen?' she choked into the silence. 'I spent eighteen months pretending to myself that you weren't the sexiest man alive and that my feelings for you were strictly platonic, but the way you took care of me during my illness…' She closed her eyes to hold back another wave of tears and tried with all her might to stop her voice from breaking. 'How could I not have fallen in love with you after that? And loving you has changed everything for me. A family of my own has always been a distant thing and now I find myself longing for it, and I'm longing for it with *you*. I want to spend the rest of my life with you and have your children and raise a family…'

Pain flaring in his eyes, he snatched hold of her wrists and pressed his forehead to hers. 'Bella, if I could give it to anyone it would be you. But I can't.'

She'd known it, but to hear it from his own mouth hurt more than she could ever have believed.

The nugget of hope her heart had held onto even when her brain had been telling it not to be so foolish shattered, and she finally crumbled.

Marcello could never allow himself to love her.

'I know you can't, and that's why I have to go,' she sobbed.

He shook his head despairingly. 'You *don't* have to go. We can—'

'I *do*. I don't want to leave you, Marcello, you must know that. Working for you has been the most infuriating but fulfilling time of my entire life and if I could stay by your side as your right-hand woman for ever then I would, but I *can't*. I can't be around you with these foolish dreams. I can't work by your side waiting for the day you start dating again and have my heart broken all over again.'

He palmed her cheeks and caught her tears in his thumbs, then pressed his forehead to hers again. 'I never wanted to break your heart, *bella*.'

'You're not breaking it, Marcello—I'm breaking it all by myself. You gave me every warning and I tried to listen but there was nothing I could do to stop it. I know you care for me and I know this is hurting you too, and I'm so sorry, and I'm sorry but I can't go to Rome with you.'

The scratching in Marcello's throat had spread to his chest. She could have been ripping at them with her nails.

The disaster he'd sensed coming when he'd recognised the attraction in her stare had detonated around him, and for the second time in his life, the solid foundations of his world were cracking around him.

'You want to leave me now?' he asked, still hardly believing. Not wanting to believe. Still half waiting for Victoria to break into a smile and tell him this was all one big joke.

'I don't want to leave you at all but I have to. Please try to understand. I will work until the end of the week to get everything in order but I can't do Rome. I just don't think I could bear to watch you act normally when I know the memories will be ripping you to pieces and the comfort I'll want to give you… It's just too much. Please understand. Please.'

The thick weight in his guts was pulling him under, a darkness in his bloodstream steadily creeping through his pores and deepening with every passing second. His nightmare a reality.

The best person in his life. He was losing her.

He was losing Victoria. And it was all his own fault. He'd sensed the danger. Not just sensed it. Known it.

He could make threats. Legal threats. Financial threats. Deploy all the weapons in his arsenal to make her stay and keep her by his side for ever.

'I understand,' he whispered hoarsely.

And that, for him, was the worst part. He *did* understand. He'd fled Rome and made Manhattan his home to escape his own pain, and because he understood it, he had no choice but to let her go.

He could never give her what she needed. What she deserved.

He should have walked away when he still had the chance.

'I will not make you work any of your notice period. We can say goodbye to each other now.'

Her face contorted. 'Thank you.'

The bleakness in his stare felt like a knife in Victoria's heart, and she tightened her hold on his cheeks and pressed her lips wet with tears to his.

His hands burrowed into her hair and his lips parted as they shared a kiss of such tender passion the anguished scream from her heart that this would be their last had her clinging tightly to him and scraping her fingers through his hair, imprinting his taste and scent into her memories to see her through a lifetime.

Letting him go was a physical wrench but it had to be done. Every minute longer that she stayed only prolonged the agony.

In silence, she gathered the last of her possessions and walked to the door.

He made no effort to follow her. Neither of them needed to say it was better that way.

'I'll email Audrey when I get back to the apartment,' she said quietly. She didn't add that her resignation was already written. Only that now-smashed nugget of hope had stopped her pressing send before.

What a foolish, foolish thing to hope for.

He closed his eyes and nodded.

She swallowed. 'Thank you for taking such good care of me and for everything you've taught me.' She had to catch a breath to continue. 'Thank you for being the best person in the world… I will carry you in my heart for ever.' The tears almost blinding her, she wiped them away so she could look at Marcello's beautiful face one last time and give the thanks that meant the most. 'And thank you for remembering my name.'

The smile he conjured was only a ghost of the heart-breaking smile she loved so much but it shattered her heart into a thousand pieces.

Hoarsely, he said, ‘As if I could ever have forgotten it.’

CHAPTER TWELVE

MARCELLO ATE THE last of his surprisingly bland breakfast bagel, screwed the wrapping into a ball, and aimed it at the wastebin he kept in the corner of his office for this express purpose. 'In one,' he preened with a fist-pump.

But there was no droll, 'Congratulations,' to follow.

There hadn't been for four days.

There was only him.

Only him, and he had an investment pitch to prepare for.

About to buzz Ryan into his office, there was a knock on the door and Ryan walked in.

Ryan was Victoria's trial replacement, recommended by Victoria in her official resignation letter. Marcello was prepared to give him a chance at filling Victoria's shoes but was not yet ready to have him occupy her desk.

He didn't think he would ever be ready to see someone else occupying the space she'd made her own.

'Excellent timing,' he said. 'I was about to call you. Can you prepare a report on Symon Tech for me?'

'It's already done, sir.'

'Good work,' he said, impressed.

Ryan looked sheepish. 'I didn't do it.'

He swallowed against the automatic tightening of his throat. 'Victoria?'

Four days on and saying her name hadn't got any easier.

The younger man nodded. 'I'll email it to you.'

'Thank you.' He let a beat of silence pass. When that wasn't filled, said, 'I presume there was something you wanted from me?'

'Yes. Err… A few of us have, err, been, err…'

He had to fight his eyes from rolling. Victoria *never* prevaricated. 'Get to the point.'

'We've organised a whip-round to buy Victoria a leaving gift,' Ryan blurted out.

This time the whole of Marcello's body tightened.

'And you are wanting me to contribute?' He was already pulling his wallet out of his suit jacket pocket. In a digital world, Marcello never felt comfortable unless he had a wedge of cash on him. He pulled out five one-hundred-dollar bills.

Ryan's eyes widened.

'Anything else?' Marcello asked when the man who wished to fill the indispensable Victoria's shoes continued hovering.

'Would it be okay for me and Cate to finish early today so we can buy her the gift? We were going to buy it over the weekend but we've just learned she'll be gone by then.'

'Gone where?' he asked casually.

'Back to Ireland. Dani called her. She's flying home tomorrow evening. Ideally we want to drop the gift to her apartment tonight.'

His heart contracted then pulsed with ice that spread into his every crevice.

Fingers digging into the mahogany of his desk, Marcello inclined his head and, through a smile he had to use imaginary marionette strings to pull off, said, 'Do you know what you are going to buy her?'

'We did but her leaving means we need to rethink it.'

'She likes to wear rose-gold jewellery. Do you have a card for her?' he added in case Ryan was tempted to ask how Marcello knew the kind of jewellery Victoria liked to wear. He wouldn't have been able to answer. It was just something he knew.

'Yes, sir.'

'Good. Bring it to me to sign and send me the report, and then you and Cate can leave. Take the day.'

Ryan's eyes widened again.

'And, Ryan?'

'Yes, sir?'

'If I have to tell you one more time not to address me as sir, I will open up recruitment for the role. *Capisce?*'

Ryan gave an uncertain smile and nod.

'*Bene.* If you ever meet my father you can address *him* as sir. Now get me the card and the Symon Tech report.'

Alone again in his office, Marcello blinked sharply, breathed deeply, and pulled his schedule up on his computer. He had a flight of his own tomorrow evening, to

Rome, but there would be no chance of bumping into Victoria at the airport. Flying privately was a whole different experience from flying commercial.

The schedule before him had been inputted entirely by Victoria, who always thought and worked ahead. Her efficiency meant he was yet to let Ryan loose on it. Her efficiency meant that only her physical presence had been missed. He noted that meetings that had been arranged for the week the storm had shut Manhattan down had all been rearranged. She must have done it the afternoon he'd fallen asleep.

He took a deep breath to loosen the painful tightening in his chest. He was having to do that a lot.

A message pinged. The Symon Tech file.

Usually he would get Victoria to print off two copies, one for each of them to read through. Get her to write her thoughts in the margins. Compare notes. By the time they met with the company seeking his investment, he would have a good idea if he wished to go ahead with it. He was always open to changing his mind—you needed to meet the people behind the company before solidifying if you wished to invest with them. After all, he'd gone to the Hansons pitch two years ago thinking he would likely invest, but the directors had proved themselves to be such terrible people that their staff had deliberately sabotaged the pitch.

Cretins was what Victoria often referred to the directors of Hansons as. Cretins. Delivered in that Irish lilt that always put a smile on his face.

He was quite sure that in another week or so he'd be able to smile again without having to use imaginary marionette strings. One day soon, he hoped to remember her smile without having to struggle for breath.

Victoria hurried up the stairs to her apartment being careful not to squeeze her coffee cup too tightly and have the hot fluid spill over her hand.

Catching her breath, she unlocked the door and put her pastrami wrap and coffee on the small kitchen table. The washing had finished. She chucked the contents into the dryer then put her towels into the washing machine. That would be her last load. If she hadn't overslept, it would already be done. But she had overslept, mainly because she'd still been awake at three a.m. willing her body to go to damned sleep.

She estimated she had just enough time for the towels to dry and for her to lob them in the suitcase before the car came to take her to the airport.

A car Marcello had arranged for her.

Not that he'd told her of it himself. Audrey had done that when Victoria had gone to the office the day before to hand in her company credit card and complete the company exit form. She'd timed it for when she knew Marcello would be in a meeting. She was functioning with what felt like all her limbs missing and a heart that had forgotten how to beat a normal rhythm. Just to imagine entering the skyscraper knowing he was under the same roof as her made blood pound in her head. Made it pound everywhere. She was holding up well enough, just focussing on tying up everything that needed tying up before she flew home to her family. To see him again would destroy that. She only had so much strength. Getting through each day was as much as she could cope with.

Before she'd left though, Audrey had asked what time she needed to be at the airport because 'the boss' had instructed Audrey to arrange for a Guardiola Group car and driver to transport her.

Victoria had no idea how she'd kept her legs upright or how she'd managed to answer without breaking down.

One day at a time had become a mantra, and she repeated it now while she forced her stomach to accept food it recoiled from. She managed half the wrap before binning the rest and dragging herself to the bedroom to clean the windows. She would give the apartment keys to the driver. If—and this was a big if—Ryan proved himself to Marcello and was given the job permanently, the keys would be passed to him.

On the bed lay her opened suitcases. Already packed in one was the Tiffany box containing a rose-gold bracelet that she'd been gifted from her colleagues. It was exquisite. It must have cost a fortune. Ryan, Cate and Dani had come to the apartment the night before with takeout and given it to her then, along with a giant leaving card. It had been a wonderful gesture and a wonderful evening, even if she'd had to deflect as to why she'd resigned and was moving back to Ireland. Missing her home was the excuse she'd used. She had the impression none of them believed her.

Was she doing the right thing? Running from her life and back to the home where she'd always felt like the cuckoo in the nest? Adapting to life in America had been hard but once she had adapted, it had been wonderful. New York was home.

But it had taken Marcello to feel like that. Taken Marcello to make her feel wanted. Needed. Remembered. To bring her to life and step into being the woman her teenage self had so longed to be, all long before they'd become lovers. And he hadn't even tried.

And now he was tied to everything. There was not a single aspect of her life he hadn't weaved his way into.

Although she'd promised herself to leave it until she was back in her childhood bedroom, she sat on the bed and reached into the case for the leaving card. She'd opened it in front of her expectant ex-colleagues but had only skimmed the hundreds of messages and signatures crammed into the white space. Now, she pored over it, searching, searching…

And then she found it. No bigger or smaller than any of the others it was nestled amongst.

Best wishes in wherever life takes you. Marcello.

A tear rolled down her cheek and landed with a plop on the card. It was the first tear she'd shed since leaving his apartment… Horror gripped her to realise the tear had landed on his name, and she dabbed frantically at it with her sleeve. Her efforts only made it worse. She'd smudged his name and his message. Smudged the one thing created by his hand that she had to take with her.

With a howl of anguish, she rolled into a ball and sobbed.

Marcello paced his office. Could not stop pacing. Kept looking out of the window over the Manhattan skyline. The fresh snow that had been falling on his drive to the office had stopped. The skies were clearing. Soon he would be up there in it. In two hours he would be on his way to the airport, on his way to Rome. In one hour and thirty minutes, Victoria would step into a company car and be taken to the same airport for a flight to the same continent but to a different country and for purposes that were the reverse of the same coin.

She was flying from pain. He was flying to it. And he wouldn't even have her by his side to...

He stopped pacing abruptly.

A wave of revulsion at the direction his thoughts had tried to take washed through him.

Dio, he was despicable.

Was he seriously trying to suggest to himself that he'd only agreed to Benito's request because he'd subconsciously thought having Victoria there would make it bearable?

There was a knock on his door quickly followed by it opening and Ryan stepping in.

'It is customary to wait for an affirmative response before entering a room,' Marcello snarled.

The shock on Ryan's face brought him up short.

Running his fingers through his hair, he took a deep breath. 'I apologise.'

'No, my fault,' Ryan said, backing out of the office.

A sudden image of Victoria backing into his apartment's elevator flashed before him. The smiling wave she'd given him.

'Ciao, amigo.'

'Amigo is Spanish.'

'I know.'

'You can't quit over a bagel.'

'I just did.'

Suddenly he found himself unable to draw breath. The walls of his office were closing in on him, perspiration breaking out over his skin.

'Sir?'

Ryan's voice broke through.

Marcello looked at the young man doing everything he could to impress and prove he could replace Victoria.

But no one could replace her. No one could even come close. Not in any aspect of his life.

Head spinning, the walls crowding ever closer, he headed to the door. He needed air.

Travelling the elevator to the ground floor with no memory of getting in it, he stepped from the lobby into the crisp winter daylight of the pedestrian plaza his building faced. People going about their business at the end of the working day. Workers with their heads down. Tourists with their phones out snapping photos.

A young father in unsuitable winter clothes holding the hand of a toddler dressed in a snowsuit…

'You can't quit over a bagel.'

'I just did.'

He put a hand to his chest and tried to pull air into his uncooperative lungs.

The child stumbled. The father scooped him up. Marcello couldn't tear his gaze from them.

Livia floated in his vision.

'You are allowed to move on too, Marcello.'

'I'm good.'

He closed his eyes. Opened them. The father was still carrying his toddler. He stared after them until they disappeared from sight.

He'd not been *good* since he'd touched his son's forehead and panicked to feel the heat coming from it.

He'd run from the pain but had never run from Tommaso. He carried his child with him. A piece of him. He'd given the whole of his heart to his son and would never betray his memory and the purity of his love by letting anyone else in to share it. Would never open himself to pain again.

But pain had found its way back to him.

Pain and loss. Deeper than he could have believed he was still capable of feeling after Tommaso.

Work hard and play hard, that was what he'd dedicated himself to. Because life was fragile. Fleeting. You could close your eyes to the night and never see another sunrise, and all that would be left of you was an emptiness in the souls of those who'd loved you that nothing could fill.

Or so he'd believed.

It hadn't been his office walls closing in on him, it had been the world. His world. His world without Victoria.

She was his world. His everything.

He raised his head, closed his eyes and spoke a prayer to his son.

And then he went back into the lobby and spoke to the nearest doorman. 'I need a car. Now.'

At Marcello's second stop, he jumped out of the car and slid through the slush to the door. On the side of it a list of apartment numbers but no names.

He'd never visited the apartment before. Had no idea what number it was.

Swearing loudly, he called Ryan. The car for Victoria would be arriving at any moment.

The tumble dryer beeped at the same moment Victoria's intercom rang.

She closed her eyes.

So this was it, then.

Dully, she pressed the button to open the entrance door. She'd been told the driver would carry her cases to the car. Her life, all packed away. All except three towels. She could only hope they'd actually dried.

She supposed the towels being a little damp wouldn't

matter. It wasn't like her parents didn't have a washing machine or anything.

She wouldn't stay with them for long. That much she'd decided. She had her nest egg plus the extra three months' salary unexpectedly credited to her bank account only that morning. Marcello generous to the very end, and now she could easily afford to put down a deposit on a home of her own. Maybe afford to buy a home for herself outright. Maybe ask Grandma Brigit if she'd like to move in with her. At least her dragon breath would keep Victoria warm and her sharp tongue keep her on her toes. Stop her falling into the pit of despair she was so close to the edge of. The tears she'd wept earlier had been a temporary stem on the pain but she was barely clinging on.

Her decision had never felt so real as it did in that moment.

In a few hours she would no longer share the same sky as Marcello and she was going to have to find a way to live with that.

Although expected, the knock on her door made her jump. She hadn't moved from the intercom.

Pulling herself together, she yanked the door open, took one look at the man standing there and, with a whimper, reflexively closed it.

Adrenaline shooting through her, hand over her mouth, she staggered backwards.

The voice she loved was faint through the reinforced safety door.

'Please, *bella*, let me in.'

She shook her head frantically as if he could see her, the only word in her head an echoing *no*.

Not now. Not when she'd spent the whole week fighting the craving to seek him out and tell him she'd changed her mind, that she would rather suffer twelve-hour days by his side knowing he would never love her than spend another second without him.

She'd never understood what it felt like to miss someone before. Truly miss them, as an ache in her very soul.

She understood it now.

'I know this is terrible timing but there are things I need to say to you, and I want to say them to *you*, not to a door. Please let me in.'

Shaking inside and out, she stared through the blinding tears at the door.

After she'd wiped the tears, it took a burst of impetus to make her body move and open it.

Bright but dull blue eyes captured hers. Broad shoulders rose. 'Thank you.'

It hurt to even look at him.

Turning her face, she whispered, 'I'm leaving in a few minutes.'

He closed the door.

She heard him take a deep breath. 'I know, and I'm here to beg you not to go.'

The howl that echoed in the room came from her own throat.

'Please, *bella*, come back to me,' he begged. 'Don't go. Come back. I can't function without you.'

Her heart and stomach plummeted to her toes. Ryan had confided that he was finding it hard to gel with Marcello and that he believed it obvious Marcello thought him a poor replacement for her.

Stumbling to the tumble dryer, she groped for the towels and hugged them tight to her chest. She had no idea how she made her mouth work. 'Look, Marcello, I know Ryan can be a little earnest but he has great—'

'Not as my EA,' he interrupted.

She blinked hard.

He stepped over to her and gently took the towels she was using as a shield from her arms, and placed them on the edge of the table. Then he gazed down at her and, with a long sigh, stroked her cheek. 'Victoria, I want you to stay with me as my wife. I want to marry you.'

His words were such a shock that it took a long moment to fully absorb them.

Absorbing them only added to the distress.

Swiping at his hands, she backed away from him so quickly that she bashed into the table.

'I never thought you were capable of such cruelty,' she cried. 'To play on my feelings like this, just because you can't adjust to having—'

The precariously placed towels fell to the floor. With them fell a glittering ring.

Marcello watched Victoria's gaze fall on the ring he'd raced back to his apartment to get and had held tightly the whole way to her, the ring he'd forgotten he was holding the moment he'd looked at her for the first time in what felt like a whole life. He must have let go of it when he'd taken the pile of towels from her without even realising.

Crouching down in the stunned silence, he picked it up then slid onto his knees before her and gazed at her until her wide eyes slowly turned back to him.

It killed him to see the misery contained in them. The redness ringing them. The dullness of her complexion.

He took hold of her hand. It was cold.

'I love you, *bella*,' he said quietly. 'That is why I want you to stay. I want you to come back to *me* because I cannot live without you.'

Her chin was wobbling. Her beautiful little chin with the faint little cleft.

He tightened his hold on her hand. 'I never forgot you because you caught me spellbound the moment I saw the look on your face at the final piece of sabotage your old colleagues did for that pitch. I carried that look with me for months. I carried your name. I gave Denise a maternity package my finance team told me I was mad to give but I did not care, and do you know why?'

She gave the smallest shake of her head.

'I did not care because deep down I knew it meant she would never come back and that I could bring you in as her replacement.'

She sucked in a small breath.

He smiled wanly and kissed her fingers. 'All this

time, Victoria. I have loved you all this time and I was too damned blind and too damned scared to see it. I let you go and sabotaged my own happiness because I thought there was no room left in my heart, but you are in there with him, and I swear to you, there is room in there for all the children you want to have with me. I want them too.' Tears filled his eyes, and he shook his head, still hardly able to believe the truth and the depth of his feelings. 'It has taken me eleven years to learn that although the past cannot be changed, the future does not have to be stuck there. You…' He sighed and kissed her fingers again. Was he imagining that they were warming…?

Keeping hold of her hand, he spread her fingers out and slid the ring on her wedding finger. 'This belonged to my grandmother. My grandfather gave it to me over Christmas. He knew—my whole damn family knew—that my heart had opened for someone…you…but that I needed the push to open my eyes.'

He smiled again at the widening of *her* eyes. 'I needed the push. All the pushes. My heart knew but the rest of me refused to see, and now it is all I can see and all I can feel. I have run from pain before but I cannot run from this…there is nowhere for me to run to. I do not know what the spell is you have cast on me but you have brought me back to life. I can get through anything if I have you with me. You are in my heart and my soul—you *are* my soul. My soul mate. You make each day a joy to live. Stay with me, please. Forgive me for being so blind, and stay with me for ever and let me love you the way you deserve to be loved, which is entirely for yourself because you are the best person in the world and just to see your face is enough to make my heart sing. Please, Victoria, stay with me. Marry me.'

Warm fingers tentatively touched his head and then slid down his cheek as she sank to her knees. 'Say it again,' she whispered.

'Which part?'

'The part about loving me.'

He gazed deep into the hazel eyes he would love for ever. 'I love you.'

A tentative smile. 'Again.'

'I love you.'

A wider smile. 'One for luck.'

Laughter broke free and he kissed her. 'I love you.'

Victoria wound her arms around Marcello's neck and stared in wonder at the face that had become the most beloved face in the whole of her world. 'I thought I would never see you again.'

'Forgive me. I never wanted to cause you pain.'

'I know,' she said softly. She'd always known what she meant to him but had never dared believe he would allow his heart to open enough to embrace it.

To feel the embrace of his love… She expelled the happiest sigh of her life. 'I love you, Marcello.'

'And I love you.'

'Say it again.'

'I love you.' He cupped her cheek and kissed her

deeply. 'Marry me and I will show it and say it every day for the rest of my life. Marry me and let us spend every day of the rest of our lives together.'

'I like the sound of that.'

'Then you will marry me?'

'As soon as we can.'

She didn't just see his smile but felt it right in her heart.

'I like the sound of *that*.' He kissed her again. 'Victoria Guardiola. My wife and business partner.'

'Business partner?'

A slow nod and smile, all without the tip of his nose leaving hers. 'Everything I have is yours. Let us take on the world together.'

Their next kiss was so deep and passionate, and the joy bursting from Victoria's heart so loud, that she failed to hear the intercom buzz, announcing the driver's arrival.

It didn't matter. She was exactly where she was meant to be.

EPILOGUE

JESSICA PUSHED HER great-grandfather's wheelchair onto the back lawn of the sprawling garden. Keeping pace with them, her sprightly great-grandmother.

The snow had fallen hard overnight. To Jessica's mind, snow like this, rare though it was, was no playground for the elderly. Her great-grandparents, though, were no one's idea of elderly. At the first hint of snow, they insisted on getting out there and enjoying it like children. According to Jessica's grandmother, they had always been like this. Ninety-four and eighty-three respectively, they wore their ages loosely.

Wheelchair parked, Jessica helped her great-grandfather to his feet. She always had the sneaking feeling he got a kick out of getting her or one of her siblings or cousins to push him around as he was actually pretty nimble on his feet. The one time she'd suggested he might be faking his occasional lack of agility, his blue eyes had emitted such a twinkle that she'd understood why her great-grandmother had fallen in love with him all those decades ago.

Her great-grandmother, from whom Jessica had inherited her red hair, smiled at her husband as she slipped her arm into his. Her hair now pure white, the lines etched on her aged face suited her. You didn't have to look hard at her great-grandmother to see the young woman who'd captured her great-grandfather's heart.

With a wistful ache in her belly and chest, Jessica watched them walk companionably to the bench in the section of the garden they'd created to remember those they'd loved and lost through the years, including the baby who would have been her great-uncle. They both kicked the snow as they walked. She watched them sit together, gloved hands clasped tightly, her great-grandmother's cheek resting on the side of her great-grandfather's shoulder, chatting in that easy way they always did that often sounded like it was in their own particular language. So taken was she by the strange yet beautiful sight of a love that had lasted for generations that she didn't notice the snowball hurtling towards her until it smacked into her shoulder.

It was impossible to tell which of her great-grandparents had thrown it—they were both doubled over with the familiar shared laughter Jessica knew she would never settle for anything less than when she found her own soul mate.

* * * * *

Were you swept off your feet by
Resisting the Bossy Billionaire*?*

Then don't miss these other dazzling stories
by Michelle Smart!

Christmas Baby with Her Ultra-Rich Boss
Innocent's Wedding Day with the Italian
Cinderella's One-Night Baby
The Forbidden Greek
Heir Ultimatum

Available now!